Alpha and Bear

Apex Investigations: Book Four

Julia Talbot

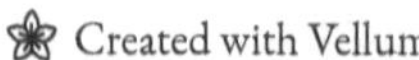 Created with Vellum

Contents

Alpha and Bear

Wolf shifter PI Mick Hartness is sick to death of being on the bad side of a criminal who wants him and his whole team dead. Now, with the help of the cops and the feds, Apex Investigations Inc. is closer than ever to reeling the guy in and getting back to living life without hiding. But that means Mick needs all of his mixed pack on deck and ready to fight, including their youngest member, bear shifter Kit, who Mick has the softest spot for.

Kit is sure his skills can help not only catch their nemesis, but help take some of the stress of running the agency off Mick. Too bad Mick will never see him as anything as a kid who needs to be protected. Which is why Kit decides to strike out on his own and get a job that allows him to do more than take pictures of cheating husbands and keep the motor pool running.

The thought of losing Kit finally makes Mick ready to show Kit how he really feels; that kit his mate. Can he keep Kit with him and also catch a killer who's becoming more and more dangerous everyday? Or will Mick lose everything he holds dear?

Apex Investigations Reading Order

Fox and Wolf

Jaguar and Grizzly

Mountain Lion and Bobcat

Alpha and Bear

For Cinders and Deborah and Elke and all the ladies and gents on my group who urge me on and, as always, to my wife, BA

Acknowledgements: To Jason and Jaymi for keeping my words as in line as you can, and to Kanaxa, whose covers have made this series more than the sum of its parts. Thank you.

ONE

Mick Hartness looked around the big lounge at the Apex office, shaking his head.

Ever since Carrie had gone virtual and then quit, not wanting the danger of coming to the office and needing to take care of her ailing mom, Mick was realizing how much their admin wolf had cleaned up after them. Jesus, his PIs were pigs.

Apex Investigations was thriving again in spite of their crazy stalker nemesis or whatever they had. The jury was still out there as far as what he would do next, but they'd had a raft of shit, and they'd all been sick to death of walking on eggshells.

His tech man, James, was still working that conspiracy theory angle, but everyone else was working a regular case. Which meant everyone was coming to the lounge to eat, dropping the trash where they stood, and getting back to work.

Shaking his head, Mick picked up a pizza box, grimacing when a piece of desiccated pizza thumped around in it.

"Hey, boss," someone said softly from behind him. Not that he hadn't known their resident black bear shifter was there. He seemed to notice everything about Kit these days. "You need some help?"

"You mind? This place stinks." Literally. It smelled like spoiled food and dirty socks.

"Of course not. I have a trash bag. I can smell it from my office." Of course Kit could. Bears put wolves to shame where noses were involved.

"Good man." Mick gave Kit an approving grin. "I swear to god, Dylan and Hank are filthy."

"Ex-cops," Kit said sagely. "You should see their vehicles."

"No thank you." Mick rolled his eyes. "So bears?"

"Fastidious. Trust me. We only have so much room to hibernate."

"Good to know. I guess if you have to live in a cave..."

Kit wrinkled his nose. "I like my king-size bed."

Mick was surprised to feel a tightening in his lower body at thinking of Kit in his bed. Damn.

Kit winked at him, dark eyes dancing with mirth. "I'm not a cave bear. I'm a Denver bear."

"You are. All video games and dorky movies." He chuckled, thinking of the kid Kit was when they'd met. He'd been so self-contained and awkward but eager to learn.

"Not all." Kit shrugged, looking down. "Not all games."

"Hey. You're amazing." He stopped the "kiddo" that wanted to pop out. Kit had asked him to stop calling him that, and Mick was trying his damnedest. "Come on. Let's do this clean up shit, and I'll make pancakes."

"Oh. You'll cook for me?"

It was usually the other way, but Mick made an empowering pancakes and bacon for late-night supper.

"I will. I'd love to. It's been a while since it was just the two of us for pancakes." He adored how Kit enjoyed his food. It made him feel like he was ten feet tall and bulletproof. Hell, Kit was the one to make him feel that way most of the time.

"I'd like that, Mick." No *boss* now. Just Mick. "Let's get to it."

Mick nodded and got to work. If he got to have late-night pancakes with Kit, he couldn't even mind the mess.

Even if he did work with slobs.

———

Kit sat in his POS sedan pretending to play with his phone while he took pictures of this lady who was having an affair with a roller derby queen. Her husband wanted the photos to take to the lawyer.

He hated the cheating gigs, but so did everyone else, so as the lowest investigator on the totem pole, he got them. Even though he'd worked for Mick longer than Brock and Grizz. And James. And Hank. Also Rey. Pretty much the whole crew except Dylan, who'd been there from the start.

Yay.

He was always going to be the lowest.

He was the youngest. He'd never been a cop or a black-ops guy. And James and Rey didn't work in the field.

The thing was, most of the time, that was okay with him. He was the getaway driver, the team medic, and the muscle a lot of times. That was all okay. This was boring as watching paint peel.

Still, he shouldn't bitch. He had a job. He had an apartment. He got to work with the man he had been in love with since he was of age.

He was a lucky guy.

Kit rolled his eyes as the ladies went for round three. Would they notice if he had Uber Eats deliver to the car? Probably. His belly rumbled. Did he have another honey nut granola bar in the glove compartment?

A quiet tap came to his window, scaring the hell out of

him. Then fellow investigator Rey's lean face appeared out of the shadows.

"Whoa." He rolled down the window. "Rey?"

"Hey! I brought you Burger King, and I have the new D&D podcast for us to listen to. Let me in!"

Kit unlocked the car, and Rey slipped in. "Thank god. I was starting to go a little stir crazy. I have all the pics I could ever need, but the client expensed me to stay the whole time they were together."

"Dylan has a stakeout, too, so I asked him to drop me off so we could hang out." Rey was the bestest best friend in explored space.

"You rock. I have a handheld Nintendo too." He'd been saving the battery, but Kit would burn it for Rey. He unwrapped his burger. "You eat with Dylan?"

"I did. I have Ding Dongs for later to share. How long can they possibly have sex?"

Kit rolled his eyes. "This is round three. Round. Three."

"Wow. That's kind of amazing for love in the afternoon." Rey's coppery-colored eyes twinkled.

"Right?" The burger was perfect. Greasy with just the right amount of mayo. "God, you rock. Thanks again. You can hook your phone into the radio so we can listen to the podcast, if you want."

The fox knew him better than anyone—they had bonded over Dr. Who and Asimov and David Eddings, and together they had discovered Eric Asher and Fortnite.

"Cool." Rey leaned on him. "I needed my bear time."

"Uh-huh. I'm way more fun on stakeout than Dylan."

Rey chuckled while he nodded. "He gets all growly wolf."

"Which cool in the bedroom, less fun at work." Kit chuckled softly. Not that he'd know, really.

He hadn't actually...had real-life experience with growly or otherwise in the bedroom. He'd watched a lot of porn...

"Yeah. He's really kind of set in his ways, and he has his methods." Rey wrinkled his nose. "In the office, we can mesh. In the car on a stakeout? Ugh." Rey shuddered.

"Rough, huh?" He chuckled softly. "You're always welcome to hang with me, you know?"

"Thanks, Kit. It's nice to get out of the office sometimes."

"You see things I never would," Kit said, and he meant it.

"Yeah. And you see a lot." Rey leaned harder. "Thanks for letting me play with you."

"Anytime, honey. No one else seems to want to."

Rey raised an eyebrow. "Don't be too sure. Some things just take time."

Kit snorted. Right. He'd thought for a little while after he asked Mick to stopping calling him a kid that Mick was looking at him in a new way. But he just didn't know now. It had all...gone back to Mick treating him like he was a kid.

Maybe he wasn't desirable. It happened. But he knew Mick was his mate, one way or the other. He could be happy with that.

Or maybe he just needed to hit Mick with a shovel. He chuckled, and Rey poked him. "Play a game with me."

"You got it." He checked the target again, but they were very, very busy, so he grabbed the Nintendo.

They could get some good gaming time in while the ladies smashed the record for go-arounds.

Mick headed out to the Sapp Brothers truck stop, needing to meet with an informant about a client, and then he'd have lunch with Greg Douglas, who was a good friend of his on the police force. He needed to check in on all the shit that had gone down with a tiger shifter who had tried to kill them all and had ended up dead, but Greg thought his office at the precinct was compromised.

The world was insane. He thought it always had been, but it was worse now than ever. At least personally.

He was torn between protecting his team and letting them back out into the world to do their jobs. He was attracted to Kit, maybe even mated to him from the way he'd been feeling, but he also felt weird as shit about that. He'd taken Kit in as a teenager. Should he be lusting after the guy even if he was all grown up?

Kit was way too young for him, but there was something about the bear that suited him to the bone and it was getting harder and harder to fight.

Mick pulled off I-25, sliding into the back parking lot at Sapps. This was for a client, and he was meeting a truck driver who supposedly had some information about a stolen load of electronics. Hopefully routine.

His phone beeped, the text coming in to say, <semi coming in off the hwy. Look alive.>

<I'm here.> He did love his tech team and how they could keep him informed almost anywhere he was. James was the man. His computer kitty knew all, saw all.

<name is Timothy Greenfield, nickname Tank, drinks Dr Pepper and Red Bull.>

<Got it.> He would get the man a drink and some snacks, make nice. That seemed to go over well with these guys. Just like it did with cops and PIs.

Hell, Mick was a huge believer in offering respect to everyone. He knew that people responded to that basic decency, and if they didn't, then something was wrong.

<On my way in.> That way Tank didn't see him come out of a pickup and not a rig in case he wasn't the informant and they had it wrong.

Mick had the man's picture, his habits, and a vague idea of the information he was looking for. All he had to do was wait.

As soon as the guy came in, Mick slipped in behind him at the Coke cooler, browsing along. He was willing to be easy and not push unless he thought he was losing his chance.

If the last few years had taught him anything, it was to be careful, to watch his back. This guy knew he was meeting a PI, but Mick needed to make sure this wasn't a setup, or some kind of trap. Was he paranoid and much more cautious these days?

Hell, yes.

He dared anyone that had gone through what he had, not to be.

Tank walked over to him, grinned too wide. "Pete? Pete, bro, I haven't seen you in an eon!"

"Hey, man. How you doing? Just stopping in, or you doing the whole shower and supper thing?"

"Nah. I just wanted a Coke and a Slim Jim. Still need to walk Flash."

"I'll buy. I'd love to walk a bit with you two and stretch my legs." He thought this guy was on the up and up. He smelled honest. Thank god.

"Sounds like a plan. Seriously." Tank nodded to him, offering him a relieved glance.

Excellent. He'd read that right. Not here where someone could easily overhear. Out there where they could only hear each other. And James could keep an eye and ear on them. He had an ace in the hole that Tank here couldn't know about.

James would be recording every word, hand-feeding him intel if he needed it.

They got the drinks and jerky and headed out to the parking lot, walking slow and steady.

"Sorry, man," Tank finally said. "I want you to know what

I do, but I'm not wanting to take chances. The load I lost was pricey, and I'm in some big heat for it."

"I understand. Can you tell me what happened?"

"Yeah. I was at the Loves down there by that hotel with the nightclub? I was showering that night. Someone switched my trailer."

"When did you find out?" He could have someone pull the video from the truck stop if he had a time and date.

"Pueblo. And I passed through all my usual checks. They were really damn careful, and they targeted me specifically. They knew what I was carrying."

"So someone knew what they were doing?"

Tank nodded once, and suddenly Mick could see the hint of bear around the eyes. "Fuck yes. I've been doing this job for twenty fucking years. I've never lost a load. Not once."

"Well, for what it's worth, you might be taking heat, but the manager who hired me knows you're a good driver and a good guy. That's why I'm here."

Tank smiled. "Thanks. Let's get Flash."

Twenty minutes later, after walking the biggest basset hound he'd ever seen, Mick had all Tank could give him, Tank had another Coke and a bag of Slim Jims, and Mick was on his way to meet Greg.

The gangly raven shifter was sitting in the shadows, and it was like he was pulling the darkness around him.

"Cool effect, man," he said as he sat.

"Thanks." Greg's grin was wicked and sharp as a razor. "I've been working under the radar the last little while. It helps."

Jesus. Great. "So, what's the word?"

"It's more like no word. I've been coordinating with the Fed, Matthews. Maldinado is in the wind. No one knows where. His last passport scan shows Brazil, but you and I both know he's got dozens of fakes. Facial recognition hasn't picked him up. Hetrick is still in jail, and he's heard what happened to Patel. He keeps begging people to kill him."

So their big bad was in the wind, and the drug dealer he'd set on them last year was no longer on Maldinado's good list. Just like the tiger shifter Patel, who had kicked this all off. "We're in stasis then. Still."

"I hear you're back to work, though. Not hunkered down."

"Maybe we're trying to draw him out."

"He's a scary fucker. You considered letting the needs of the many..."

"No." No. He knew Maldinado really wanted one of his PIs, but he wasn't giving Brock up to anyone. Not a fucking chance. "He's pack."

"Hey, I get it." Greg held up his hands. "So we did all the tests; Peaches, the drug Hetrick was moving, does prove it's almost four times more effective on cat shifters. You think that's about your boy too?"

"Yes. Either directly or indirectly."

"Well, I can tell you I heard a whisper late last night that a shipment of nobenime went missing. Enough to shatter a dozen of us." Greg stared at him. "Enough to disable three times that amount."

"Christ. Okay. Okay, I'll get James on that." That was a different drug, a nerve agent, and that shit was no joke. It wiped out the will. They would all be little robots, doing Maldinado's dirty work. Mick snapped his fingers. "That's what he used on Patel."

"I'm betting on it."

Patel was a now-defunct tiger shifter who had come after Mick's team with a single-minded intensity and swamp full of croc shifters. The drug, Peaches, had taken their tech man

James down, almost to death, and had killed Patel, but he'd told Mick he hadn't wanted to go after Mick's team or hire the gators, and the nobenime would enable that. Mick believed him, even if Patel had been less than a good man.

"Well, what do you need from me?" Greg sighed and shook his head. "I feel like you're caught between the slices of a shit sandwich."

"We are. I know it's a lot, but if you could still spare us some guys."

"We have some who are volunteering to watch your place off duty."

"Thanks." That meant a lot.

"I'm going to let it slip that I'm looking to get big money fast. Desperate people seem to turn this asshole on. If he brings me in, I can work it from inside."

"No. No, this son of a bitch is diabolical." He didn't want Greg undercover in Maldinado's organization. It had almost killed their bobcat shifter Hank when he'd done the same job.

Greg's eyes were black as buttons. "So am I. And I'm not a cat."

"Man, you went from straight-arrow captain to deep in the Feds' shit in no time."

"I'm good at fitting in." Greg shrugged. "You've known me longer than most."

"Yeah." And Greg was the smartest, fiercest bird he knew. Willing to do anything to protect his flock.

"Anything you can tell me?"

He filled Greg in on Tank. "That's for Ty. I think he was working that one." Ty was another cop, one who had been friends with their resident bobcat shifter Hank when they were both on the force. "Client asked me to help find out what happened."

"People suck." Greg rolled his eyes dramatically. "Big hairy donkey dicks."

"They do. We see all of that, huh?"

"Yeah. Not just from the criminal classes."

"Oh?" Mick grinned. "Who pissed you off now?"

"The Fed. Matthews."

"Cole. What did he do?"

Greg shrugged. "He's a Fed."

"Ah." That made sense, he supposed. It was cop law—that agencies butted heads. And Greg and Cole were both a little alpha.

"Yeah..." Greg chuckled, the sound harsh and dark.

"Well, have fun with that." Their food came, and talk turned to his team and folks Mick knew on the force. Easy stuff. He actually liked Greg. The guy had a wicked sense of humor and a great love for all things shiny.

Not only that, but Greg made connections like a fiend, piecing together patterns and personalities wildly. Birdbrain.

"Are you laughing at me?" Greg asked when he grinned.

"Nope. I was thinking of a cinnamon roll."

"Yum. Get some to go. Your guys smell that on you, they'll never forgive you."

"True. At least everyone but the cats. I'll get them garlic parmesan fries."

"Yum. Okay, man. I got to head out." Greg pulled out his wallet.

"I'll expense it," Mick said, waving it off.

"I'll keep you in the loop. You see me with the bad guy, know I'm deep under."

"I will know it. We can trust you." He stood to shake hands, but he would stay long enough to order to-go food for the masses.

How did one evil son of a bitch create this much drama? How did that happen?

He guessed mastermind of crime was about the best he could describe it as, but Maldinado also had this crazy randomness. Like he was all over the place. Let's poison them, have a croc eat them...

The worst bit was the fact that Maldinado would destroy anything to get to Brock. That made him utterly unpredictable.

"Can I get you the bill, hon?" the server asked.

"Thanks. Just let me add something to go..."

———

Kit was waiting for Mick when he came in. By the main entrance. It was well protected now, with a pair of controlled doors where one only opened when the other was closed. But there were still a few waiting area chairs down in the lobby, so he sprawled, glaring at the boss when he entered.

"Wow, okay, so what did I do?" Mick asked, waving a bag he held. Which smelled like cinnamon rolls.

His nose quivered. "James says you met with Greg."

"I did." Mick raised an eyebrow. "We had lunch."

"You said you were going to meet an informant."

"I did that too. Come get your cinnamon roll." Mick headed upstairs.

His belly growled, the sound bubbling up inside him. Mick never trusted him enough to tell him things.

He wasn't a kid anymore.

Kit followed, though, because sitting in the lobby was stupid and probably did make him look like a toddler begging for crumbs. "Did you plan to tell us all what you found out?"

"Yep, but I might as well tell everyone, right?" Mick shrugged. "It's easier. How did your case go?"

"Fine. She's cheating. There are pictures. She had a lot of orgasms."

"Good for her. You said the husband seemed like a dick." Mick let himself into the lounge, and he didn't seem mad, which was nice, he guessed. And the cinnamon rolls did smell good.

"Yeah. I wish—I hope she's okay." He hated the cheating stuff.

"She'll be fine. Her new thing is a roller derby chick. She'll beat the husband down, ten to one." Mick winked. "So why are you so mad at me?"

"Because you expect us all to fill you in every time we fart, and you're meeting with the co-head of the task force on our case without letting us know." He crossed his arms, going for I-am-your-adult-and-equal.

Mick blinked, then nodded slowly. "Okay, point taken."

"Oh." He let himself drop his arms. "Thank you."

Goddess, that felt good. Just that acknowledgement that he'd had a right to be worried and upset.

"I just didn't want to get anyone stirred up if he had no news."

"Anyone meaning Brock? Since James was watching."

"Yeah." Mick started firing off texts. "I got fries and buns, enough for all."

"Then they'll come." Kit chuckled. "Always."

They were all about the food. It meant so much more than sustenance. No, with them, meals meant connecting, finding an easy way to talk without it being a formal meeting in an office.

Kit curled up in the big chair that was his. There was one that was huge, but it belonged to Grizz and Brock, the grizzly and jaguar always together.

He had a pang for a moment, and he wondered if Mick felt that way when everyone cuddled together but them. Butthead man.

Worse, what if Mick didn't feel it? What if Mick didn't care?

Okay, so that would suck so much worse than if Mick wanted him but thought he was too young.

Mick came to hand him a plate. He got fries and two cinnamon rolls. No one else's plate had that. That was something.

"Thanks." He gave Mick what he hoped was a come-hither smile and not a dorky grin.

"Of course, Kit."

The sound of his name in Mick's voice gave him shivers.

James and Hank wandered in first, sniffing the air. "Smells good."

"It is. Yummy. Swear." Kit winked at the cats, chuckling when they beelined for the fries.

They might split a cinnamon roll, but they were all about the salty and crunchy.

"Hey. Did we miss the fries?" Brock looked so sleepy, his dark hair everywhere.

"Just in time," Mick murmured.

Grizz grabbed two cinnamon rolls, rumbling a soft hello to him.

"Grizz. Brother." He smiled at his fellow bear.

Grizz leaned down to rub noses with him before heading to his and Brock's chair.

They were just missing Rey and Dylan, so he texted Rey.

<cinnamon rolls! Intel! hurry!>

<Coming! We were in the shower!>

They heard Rey and Dylan coming pretty soon after that, and they were wet-haired and more awake than the others. "Hey. Yum. Raisins." Rey headed right for the rolls.

"Thank god they showered," Hank muttered.

"At least I'm not a tomcat, pussy," Dylan shot back.

"Yeah, yeah. Just a weird, musty old wolf."

"Stakeout stale." Kit grinned. He could tease, because he got it. He had taken a twelve-day shower earlier.

"It was fun to hang out though." Rey laughed. "We were stakeout buddies."

Kit winked at him, because they'd had a ball. "Don't worry. We got all the evidence we needed."

"Not worried," Mick said. "You two are top-notch."

Warmth flooded him, and his cheeks began to heat.

Rey looked almost as pleased, but he just munched on his cinnamon roll while Dylan alternated fries and sweet.

"So?" Brock asked.

Kit waited, watching emotions play on Mick's face.

"So, there's not a hell of a whole lot to tell."

———

Mick hated to see all the guys' faces fall. Every one of them wanted this resolved.

He filled them in, from the lab tests on the Peaches drug to the stolen nobenime. "Maldinado is still in the wind, but the task force is piecing together his last movements before he really went to ground."

Grizz's arms were wrapped around Brock, holding on tight, like that would protect his mate from a drug.

"So what does that mean for us?" James asked.

"We go on like we are now."

Brock swore in Portuguese. At length. "I am tired of being in a holding pattern, *irmão*. I want to do something. Anything."

"Like what? I won't let anyone go rogue."

He couldn't. Not and allow them to get hurt.

"I could go." Kit's words fell out into the air like they belonged there.

"Go where?" Mick asked, a scowl drawing his brows down. What did Kit think he was volunteering for, exactly?

"Rogue. No one knows me. I could see if he comes for me."

"No. Hell, no. Greg is going to try to go undercover, and if that doesn't work, the Feds have another Hank on deck. No offense, Hank."

"None taken," Hank purred. "Nice to know I'm replaceable."

"None of you are replaceable," Mick snapped. "Get that through your thick skulls."

"Which is why you're out there trolling truck stops," Kit shot back. The bear was growing claws. Who would have thought?

"That's it. I'm the disposable one in my mind. I take the risks."

Brock cut the air with his hand. "I will put the word out that I want a meet with Joao. Once and for all."

Locke growled. "Are you nuts?"

"You can't, brother." James looked utterly horrified. "Please. We can't. It almost killed us before."

"Stop it." Kit stood, making them all sit back in their chairs. "We all need to stop jerking off and calling it selfless, including me. I know it's super frustrating because we've been working this so long, and he always seems to be ahead of us, but if the Feds and cops think they know where he was last, then we have James start there. Rey can poke it too. And from now on, no casework alone. Not even you, boss."

They all stared at Kit and looked as impressed as Mick felt.

Grizz nodded. "Kit is right. We're frustrated and angry, but we can't be stupid."

"Are you calling me stupid, mate?" Brock teased, but he'd relaxed obviously. His shoulders had come down from around his ears.

"Okay, then," Mick agreed. "Hank, see if you get anything different from Cole than I did from Greg. You two

worked together for ages. We all rotate out in teams. And"—
he held up a hand when Kit took a breath—"we talk to each
other."

Kit blew out his breath and nodded.

"Sounds good, boss," Dylan said. "I'm sick of stakeouts
though."

"So is Kit, I bet. I'll take the next one." He regretted the
words the minute he spoke them, but the grateful looks from
his fellow wolf and his little bear made it worthwhile.

Especially the one from Kit, which made his heart beat
faster.

Somehow his little bear had become a man. Had become
grown and mature and brave.

Mick had seen it happening, but he hadn't *noticed* it until
recently. Or maybe Kit was just letting him see it, coming out
of his shell a little more every day since he'd pulled a berserker
rage and torn the croc shifters who had tried to kill them
apart. With just his paws.

His Kit was stunning as a dire bear.

There was no one—no one on earth—that he trusted
more with his life.

"So can we relax now?" Dylan asked. "Eat our cinnamon
rolls and chill the fuck out? I want to watch the Loki series."

"Ohhh." Kit made the face. The geek face that was so
happy someone else wanted to do his thing with him.

"Yes!" James fist-pumped. "And no, Mick, you can't go
work."

"Can I snore?" He would nap. That worked for him. To
be fair to the geeks, TV in general didn't do it for him, let
alone superhero stuff.

"Yes," Kit declared. "But I will poke you if you get too
loud."

"Fair." They had all gone in to buy a new sectional a few
months back. This thing was like something out of a movie,

with three chaises and a couple of long in-between sections. Room for all, with lots of blankets and pillows.

They cuddled in together, with Rey's feet on Kit's lap, Kit solid and warm beside him.

He slid an arm around Kit, resting his cheek on Kit's head when Kit leaned on his shoulder. And about ten minutes into episode one, he was out like a light.

———

Kit stormed out of Mick's office, his hands balled into fists, his cheeks so hot they were about to go up in flames. So much for Mick taking the next stakeout. Of course Kit was going to have to do it, and Mick had asked him to see if Rey could go with him.

Just once he would like to be as important, not more but as, as Mick's something else. Anything else.

He slammed into the office Rey shared with James, throwing himself into a chair, which creaked ominously under him.

Rey gave him a cautious look. "Um. Hey. You okay?" Those copper eyes held nothing but concern for him.

"Fine. Just cooling off." In that moment, he decided he wouldn't take Rey. Fuck Mick. He'd do this on his own. In fact, he'd do this, and he'd start looking for another job.

Someone would need a bear around, right? He was a good medic, a good mechanic, a solid investigator. Someone would hire him.

He needed to find a place to live too. A job, a place to live. A car. God.

Maybe he needed to save up some. He'd lived with...on, maybe, Mick for so long.

"Hey, brother bear." James came in with a sheaf of papers, his cane in his other hand. He still had some nerve damage from the drugs that Maldinado's men had forced on, and some days he did better than others, but he was so much better. "What's wrong? You look like a thundercloud."

"That's because I'm stuck on stakeout duty. Again. I'm supposed to see if Rey—"

"Nope." James picked up the office phone and stabbed out a few numbers. "I can't spare him. Mick? What the fuck? You said you would take the next stakeout. Then you go with Kit. I need Rey here." James winked broadly at him.

Okay, that was a little hilarious.

"I'll just go alone. I don't need a babysitter."

James held up a hand. "Right. Well, it was your rule. No one goes out alone. Uh-huh. Cool. He'll meet you downstairs." James hung up. "Ta-da."

"I don't—" He sighed softly. "Can you guys help me with my resume? I think it's time for me to find another position."

"Hey!" Rey came over to grab his hands. "What does that mean? No way."

James stared at him. "I thought that, too, Kit. I did. I was so... I was sure I was gonna leave. Then I was sure I was never gonna leave again."

"I know. But—maybe it's time? I think I need to make my own way." Maybe then Mick would see him as something more than a silly little bear with no skills.

Or maybe someone would just see him.

He'd take that right now. Someone who wanted him, that touched him like he was an adult.

"Oh, honey." Rey squeezed his hands. "Don't give up on us yet."

"It's not you." He bit back the rest of the words. "I guess I need to get downstairs. Mick will be in a shit mood now, anyway."

"So poke him. Make him growl." That was James, grinning again.

"I'll think about it." Kit needed to grab a camera and a mic, just in case, and he had a go bag repacked with snacks.

He'd tell Mick he was going to work alone tonight. Mick would growl and fuss and then let him go. Mick always had something better to do. More important.

He headed down to the main lobby, and sure enough, Mick was there.

"You get the van's starter fixed?" Mick asked.

Kit gritted his teeth. "Yes. I've got this."

"Got what?"

"This assignment. I've got it. No worries." He was doing this his way, goddamn it.

Mick gave him a look. "No one goes out alone." Then he grinned. "And I did say I would take the next one, so you have to go with me."

What the fuck was he supposed to say? That he didn't want to spend time with Mick? That would be a lie. He wanted to spend hours and hours with the big alpha wolf.

A lifetime.

So he shrugged, then felt like that was a sullen teenager move, and he didn't want to be treated like one, so he had to act like an adult. "Cool. That gives me time to ply you with my ideas for upgrades to the vehicles."

"God help me." But Mick's grin widened, so he must have taken the right approach.

They headed to the van, which would work better than the sedan because the area they were working was full of delivery businesses, and they would blend right in.

Kit drove them down and parked, set the camera up where it couldn't be seen, and took a couple of establishing shots.

"So what does the client want on this one, exactly?" Kit asked. "The case file was really unclear."

"He thinks someone is stealing inventory. Wants us to

monitor comings and goings, make sure everyone who's in and out is on the shipping schedule."

That sounded like so much fun. Not.

Still, it was easy enough, and he could search on his phone while he was recording.

"So." Mick nudged him with an elbow, startling him. "Vehicles?"

Surprised, he stared at Mick. "Well, for one thing, they're woefully out of date. This may be just north of the land of crappy sedans, but we need to update at least a few of the 'gee I bought this POS at a cop auction' cars. A few to take to crappy pay-by-the-hour hotels? Sure, but we need some variety." He shrugged. "And on the ones used more often, they could use refrigerators for food and Cokes, Wi-Fi so we're not using our data."

They didn't need a thousand cars or anything, but they did need an SUV, something that fit in almost anywhere.

"You've really thought about this."

He counted to ten so he didn't snap. "It's my job. Which I'm good at." A little devil made him add, "Until I started brushing up my resume, I didn't realize how many hats I wear at Apex."

Mick did a double take. "Your resume. What the fuck are you doing that for?"

What was he supposed to say to that? "I'm just looking at my options."

Squinting, Mick pursed his lips. "Why?"

Kit sat there, shoulders coming up around his ears, not quite sure what to say. A thousand thoughts flitted through his head, but he didn't dare let them out of his mouth, and thankfully, a bay door opened at the business they were watching, and Kit took pictures of all that was going on, saving him from having to answer.

Until the guy drove off, and Mick literally poked him. "So?"

"I want to be important. I don't have to start that way. But I do want to be able to become a vital part of an organization." He didn't look at Mick, and that made it easier. "I'm not a teenager anymore, and it's time that I stop living off Apex."

Mick was silent for long moments, and he finally had to sneak a glance. Mick's face didn't give much away, but those dark eyes were burning. "You are a vital part of the organization, Kit. You're one of us. You don't need to go anywhere else."

Kit picked at the seam of his jeans. "It's great to be family, Mick. It is. But I work hard, and I want to be respected for that and not always just be assigned the most junior assignments. I think I've earned my way. So maybe I need to go somewhere else where there are more opportunities."

"I—" Mick snapped his teeth closed, then took a deep breath.

Which was, of course, when Mick's phone rang.

"Damn it." The curse was sharp, and Mick leveled a finger at him. "Hold that thought. Hartness," he barked when he answered.

Mick listened for maybe a full minute, his face going through a series of kind of extraordinary expressions. "No shit. Okay. Yeah, I'll send Hank and Dylan. Okay. And I'll get James on it. Thanks, Greg. Keep me posted until my guys get there. Bye."

"What's going on?" Kit asked.

"Pack it up, Kit. We need to get back to the office. Our drug dealer wolf Stefan Hetrick just pulled a Patel. He's out of jail. And he's dead."

"Right." He put the camera down and had them moving in less than ten seconds. Before five minutes were up, they were across town and closing in on the building.

Mick had been on the phone with James, and Kit knew from that conversation that Hank and Dylan were going to the scene because as ex-cops they could blend in, and they were on the approved list from the Fed on the task force, Cole Matthews.

He parked them and started unloading, after he checked the perimeter and made sure they were safe.

He might be the low man on the totem pole, but he knew how to prioritize. The team needed him, so he would do his job as well as he could.

Two

"Sitrep," Mick barked at James as he walked into the tech command center.

Jesus, what a fucking mess. First Kit had dropped a bomb on him about maybe leaving, which had sent him into an absolute fucking panic, and then the DB had shown up. Another fucking DB intimately tied to them and broken out of jail forcibly.

"They found him in the warehouse where we initially investigated his stuff. The cause of death is as yet undetermined." James's fingers flew on the keyboard. He had three screens scrolling with information, and Rey had two.

"When did he get sprung? What did we miss?"

"Nothing. We missed nothing. There's another dead guard." Brock paced, a deep snarl filling the air, Grizz at the door.

"Damn it. He's a wolf, not a cat. How did they get him without the damn Peaches shit?" Mick was gritting his teeth, and he fought to relax his jaw as Kit came in, raising his eyebrows.

"I'm sure it was the nobenime." That was Brock. "You

have no idea how it saps your will. You do what you're told, even as part of you is screaming to stop."

"I was thinking. Does Maldinado have a shape-shifter? Not a lycan, but I've heard stories from my family near the Four Corners..." Kit dropped that in like it was nothing.

Brock stopped pacing, staring at Kit. "We have something similar in Brazil. He might at that. He always had contacts I wanted nothing to do with. Too..." Brock waved. "Sketchy. This is how you say it, *sim*?"

Kit nodded. "If they can take on any form..."

Rey looked over. "How can we know we're safe?"

"You can hear Dylan in your head, can't you?" James asked. "We all have mates. If we can't hear them, we'll know."

Kit looked at him, then looked away. "That's good. I need to go make sure we have plenty of medical supplies."

"I don't want you wandering off." Kit couldn't hear anyone in his head. He was vulnerable, and Mick wouldn't have him getting hurt.

"I'm fine," Kit snapped, heading back out of the room, putting his feet down hard.

"Stay on it. I'll be right back." He followed Kit, waiting until they were out of earshot of the others. "Damn it, bear, I need you to stay close. I want you out of harm's way."

"Yeah? Who took the head off a croc shifter? It wasn't you. And I'm not a cat. Peaches won't get me."

"I don't want you hurt."

"Then stop doing it!" Kit roared, then stopped, eyes going wide. His cheeks went red, and he wouldn't meet Mick's eyes. "Sorry, boss. I'll check the supplies. I have my phone."

"Kit—"

"No. I need to go." Kit all but ran, and Mick cursed. Viciously. Shit, he didn't need this. Any of this.

He ducked back into the tech room. "Keep an eye on the med supply room someone."

"On it," Rey said. "Did you know he was thinking of leaving?"

The question was casual, but Mick knew better. It was too fucking timely.

He snarled, his belly full of knots. "I just learned that today."

"Me too." Rey backed off, and Brock stepped right up to plate.

"Did you learn that he loves you? Did you figure out that he's waited for you for years? That he has been doing everything on earth to prove that he's worthy of being yours?"

"Shut up."

"*Nao*. Someone needs to have a say." Brock crossed his arms over his chest. "He's loved you since he came here. You don't have to do anything about it but stop punishing him for it. He deserves credit for hard work and dedication."

"I give him the jobs we have to do!"

James cleared his throat. "You give him the least dangerous jobs because you think it's your mission to take care of him. But those are the shit jobs. You have to trust him."

"He's really talented," Rey muttered. "He cooks and cleans and fixes things. He's taking all sorts of medical classes, and he's learning how to code, even."

"I never said he wasn't amazing. Is this an intervention? We're supposed to be on the Hetrick case." Mick would grovel and beg Kit to stay. Right now, they had a finite amount of time to figure out what had happened to the damn wolf who was supposed to be in jail and maybe get a line on Maldinado's whereabouts.

"Let it go, Brock," Grizz rumbled. "You said your piece. We have work to do."

"Yeah." Brock blew out a breath but stopped to touch his arm on the way out. "I lost Locke for a long time. Don't be the fool I was, amigo."

Those soft words slid in deeper than any harsh ones could have. Asshole. He nodded to Brock and even managed a smile. "I hear you."

"Good. I am glad."

Mick sighed, noticing how Rey and James refused to meet his eyes. "Damn it. I'll go get him. Keep me posted."

"Will do, boss. We're on it." James's voice was smooth as milk.

He growled, stomping out of the room, wondering how he didn't get the luxury of getting to be grumpy about Hetrick without having to...to what? He wasn't trying to be mean to Kit, so he supposed he needed to apologize. Damn it.

He didn't have time for this shit. He honestly didn't. There was a dead man, dammit.

One that had information on his person, possibly, that was expiring as they spoke.

He headed to the supply area, listening to Kit's music, which was loud. Someone was mad. He sighed. He just felt like he was walking on eggshells.

Kit was working though. Checking inventory and marking down numbers on the clipboard.

"Hey." Mick raised his voice to be heard over the music. "Can I talk to you a minute?"

Kit gave him a quick glance, then turned the music off. "Look, boss. I apologize. I was out of line. I'm worried about the guys, is all. I'm sorry."

He tilted his head. "I'm here to apologize to you, Kit. If I made you feel like you weren't part of the team, that wasn't my intention." He clenched his hands. "You're the most important person in the world to me, and sometimes I sell you short because I have this need to keep you safe."

"I'm not a child, boss. I know you think I am, but I'm honestly not."

"I don't think you're a child." In fact, recently, he felt very adult things about Kit. "I just want to keep you safe. I'm trying. I am. But this whole damn situation hasn't helped." He held up a hand when Kit opened his mouth. "But I'll do better."

"Thank you. I'll keep my temper. I swear." Kit picked up the clipboard again. "I'll finish here, and then I'll check kitchen supplies and the warehouse supplies."

"Okay. Keep in touch with your phone in case we need to meet?"

"I will." Kit smiled. "You okay?"

"No. I'm pissed off. I want Maldinado to hit the road. Hard. Like roadkill. I keep telling myself anyone as crazy as he is has to fuck up at some point."

"He will. Eventually he will." Kit nodded to him and got back to work, basically dismissing him.

Mick stared for a long moment, then turned on his heel and left. Fuck it. He was going to his office to make calls and follow the police band and such. The big apology had come to so much BS, and he just wanted to lick his damn wounds. He was sick of feeling like a soccer ball everyone wanted to kick.

THREE

Kit kept his head down, his mouth shut, and he stayed in his room when he wasn't working. He'd made a fool out of himself, and he felt like the world's biggest fuzzy idiot.

He was pretty sure that Mal had a shape-shifter, and if he could figure something out, it would help.

Kit was digging around, hunting for something, when a hint of a story caught his eyes. A jaguar shifter that could be force-turned into a creature that could hypnotize anyone and kill them. It was a South American legend. Joao Maldinado was Brazilian like Brock, and Brock was a jaguar.

Oh god.

Kit grabbed his phone and headed out into the hallway at a run. He ran smack into Mick, who was raising his hand to knock on the door, and they both went down.

"Oof. Jesus, Kit. Where's the fire?" Mick snarled, his alpha voice in full swing.

"I know what he's done! I know why Brock!"

"Who? What?" Mick helped him stand up, then climbed

to his feet. "I was coming to get you to eat. You need to, so tell me on the way."

He grabbed Mick's hand and started pulling, his heart pounding. "There's a creature. A shape-shifter in South America. A pihulchan. It's a jaguar shifter that's been drugged, turned into a creature that can shift into anything. They hypnotize you, then they kill you! That's why he wanted Brock! To make one of those!"

Jaguar shifters were rare as hen's teeth, and Brock was powerful and smart, wild and fierce and determined.

"So...so he wants to turn Brock into some kind of super killer?" Mick shook his head. "Jesus, that's nuts. I mean, who comes up with this shit?"

"The kind of guy who uses croc shifters as henchmen and poisons cats using weasel shifters. This guy is taking away shifters' wills with drugs and using them as his own personal crime cartel." Kit waved his hands, disgusted but excited by what he'd figured out. "Not only that, but he wants *our* Brock!"

Brock stood at the door of the common kitchen. "What the hell?"

Kit rolled his eyes, dragged everyone in and explained. Slowly. Twice.

Then Brock began to curse, and James and Rey grabbed their food and headed for their laptops, their mates following.

"But I thought you said maybe he already had a shape-shifter," Mick mused. "So how is he getting into the jails?"

"His shape-shifter that he has now can look like anyone. They can walk into the jail, and until they have to talk? They're in."

"But he's not one of the jaguar things?" Mick wasn't understanding. "You mean the guy he has now does more like a glamour."

"No. No, listen. Mal took a jaguar shifter—someone like

Brock—and altered him, her, whatever. Now that person isn't himself anymore. Now he's a tool for Maldinado."

"Christ. And he still wants Brock?"

"I think at this point he just wants Brock to suffer before he dies." Kit hunched his shoulders, feeling miserable. "But just think, someone like Brock, with his skills, that can look like anyone and is totally under his control?"

"Fuck. That's why we can't get ahead."

"So what do we do?" Grizz asked.

"We fight him with me," Brock said. "If this is the case, then I need to think what I would do next."

"Except Maldinado is in control, and he's crazy."

"And a fox." Brock turned to look at Rey. "We must work together."

Kit slumped against the wall, completely worn out. Whoa.

"We can as long as you don't call me names," Rey teased. Brock had been kinda harsh to him to begin with.

"Hush, fox." Brock ruffled his hair. "No names. We'll stay close together, all of us. The apartments or the offices, and if anything else happens, we all pile in here to sleep even."

"All of us," Mick agreed, bringing Kit a plate. "Eat with me, hon."

Kiddo to hon was good, he thought. Maybe a little weird, but he would take it. Kit wanted to be lover, but they could work up to that. Right?

"I don't know if I can. I'm all adrenaline-man." He took the plate anyway, because he wasn't dead, just a little hopped up.

"Well, we'll try." Mick munched a sandwich.

"Yeah. I'm pretty good at eating, really." He ate a few chips, willing them to settle his stomach.

"You are."

A printout landed next to Mick, James tossing it at him.

"This is more coherent an explanation of the phenomenon Kit is talking about, boss."

"Hey! You guys didn't figure it out!" He was coherent, wasn't he?

"I never said we did," James deadpanned. "I just know Mick needs things simplified."

Mick flipped James off. "I get it well enough. I'll read it though."

"Yeah." Kit grinned, but he didn't feel it. He felt...sort of silly, honestly, for being so excited. He ate his sandwich and then threw his paper plate away. "I'm going to grab a shower. Night, guys."

I'm going to get wet and watch movies for a while and then jack off and go to sleep.

There was a chorus of grunts, as everyone was pretty much working on their tablets or laptops, which should be banned in the common room. He put his feet down maybe harder than he should and jumped maybe a mile when Mick grabbed his shoulder when he was a foot from his door.

"That was a good find, Kit. Don't let them make you think it wasn't."

"It's okay. I just—" *Want to go somewhere I can make a difference.* "I just want to help."

"You did." Mick pulled him into a hug, and suddenly he was fourteen again and smelling Mick for the first time and falling in love. Boom.

He shivered, and his entire body responded, a soft rumble moving through his chest.

"I need you here," Mick said against his neck, which made him shiver, made his cock harden. He couldn't bear it. What if Mick noticed?

"I don't want to go, but I want to do things to help. To be important."

Mick backed off and shook him a little. "You have no idea how you hold this whole team together."

"You don't understand, Mick. You don't get it." He didn't want to hold the whole team together.

"Then tell me what it is you want!" Mick shook him harder, fingers biting into his arms a little. Once that would have made him back down, but now it was what made him boil over.

"You! You son of a bitch! I want you!" Kit roared, slamming their chests together, and they both grunted with the impact. Then he took the only chance he might ever have and kissed Mick as hard as he could.

Mick's sound was all surprise, but the hands gripping his upper arms never let go. No, if anything, Mick yanked him closer, and the kiss went so hard and deep Kit would swear he felt his lip split.

Goddess, he would never forget this again. Never. He would always know what Mick tasted like, how they fit together.

He knew how his hard-on felt rubbing against Mick's belly, and damn if he didn't know what Mick's sexy growl sounded like, not just his frustrated one.

Mick slammed him back against his door, kissing him again, sliding his hands up to cup Kit's cheeks.

Yes. Yes! He needed this more than anything.

He reached behind him and opened his door, both of them stumbling into the dark room. He didn't want to be interrupted. Not one bit. So he locked the door when they were inside. The others could damn well knock.

Kit yanked at Mick's shirt, afraid to say something and break the spell.

Mick backed off six inches to pull it off, buttons going all over.

"Fuck." Kit reached out, growling deep as Mick pushed his hands back. "Want."

"You wait." Mick undid his pants and let them fall, and Kit stood there, mouth dry, staring. He'd seen Mick naked a lot when they all got that way to shift and groom, but this was Mick flushed and hard, his scarred body lean and strong and perfect for such a big guy. "Now you. I want to see you, hard for me."

Kit couldn't help blushing, but he pulled his shirt up and off. "I'm not hot like you."

"You're built like a brick shit house, Kit. The pants too." Mick crossed his arms over his chest and watched him, cock bobbing gently.

He refused to be embarrassed. He absolutely refused. He stripped his slacks off and stood there, his prick hard as nails.

"Fuck, I knew it. I knew you'd be rock hard and more than a handful." Mick reached for his cock, stroking it up and down.

"I want to touch. Please, Mick. I need to touch you."

"Then come and touch me, honey. I want to feel you all over me." Mick gave him a wicked, pirate smile.

Kit shivered, a hot drop of spunk sliding down his shaft. Mick did it for him, all the way. Always had, but as he'd gotten older, it had become a constant ache.

Now Mick had him in hand, and he was going to come before it even got started.

Mick slid that hand down to tug at his balls, pulling them away from his body. "Not yet, honey. Not even close."

"Sorry. I just...you're the first." And that was no lie. Mick was...it.

"Fuck. Oh, fuck, Kit. I swear I'll make you feel so good." Mick rubbed and rolled his balls, gentle but firm.

This was a fantasy. This was everything he'd ever wanted,

and he was barely hanging on by his toenails. He was going to just...die a happy fucking man.

"I got you, Kit. I get it now. You can come for me, and I'll get you up for round two. I promise." Mick was just going to kill him. Whoosh.

He would just explode.

"Mick..." He pushed up with a hard, needy kiss, demanding more, crying out as his cock nudged Mick's belly.

"Mmmhmm." The kiss scorched him, Mick grabbing his ass, rubbing them together. It wasn't enough and it was too much, and Kit cried out, his body shaking as he came over Mick's skin. "Mine... Smell so good."

Mick's growl was like a buzz saw against his soul.

Rubbing them together, Mick spread his come all over them, then started pushing him toward the bedroom, really moving him along. Not leaving, which had been his fear.

He went eagerly, dragging Mick along with him. His bed had mostly clean sheets, and he didn't think it smelled too bad.

Mick stopped to take a deep breath, then moaned. "I can smell you. Kit. It's everywhere. I want you." Mick rubbed a hand over his own belly, then grabbed his cock and stroked it.

"Please." He needed this—needed Mick to touch him. To love him. Kit dragged his fingers up along Mick's chest, letting his fingers tangle in the thick hair there.

"You're smokin' hot, Kit. Barrel chest, thighs like tree trunks, a nice, hefty cock. I could climb on and fuck you for days."

Kit whimpered. Actually whimpered. "Yes."

"Lie down." Mick pushed at him, hand on his chest. "Spread out."

He landed on his butt, coming eye level with Mick's cock. Oh, look at that. Kit licked his lips, his mouth watering. "Can I have it?"

Mick chuckled, the sound so heated, sliding down his spine. "You need that, honey? You take it and get it good and wet."

He didn't feel like Mick was thinking of him like a child—not even a little bit. They were two hungry apex predators who needed. This was hot and growly and sweaty. Kit reveled in it. He took all his considerable fantasy practice, and the occasional deep-throated banana, and went right down on Mick's cock.

Mick roared, fingers tangling in his hair as the strong hips pressed forward, pushing in deep. That cock was deceptive. It wasn't as long as his, but Mick was thick, spreading his lips, really making him work to try to get it all.

He did work at it, and he managed to swallow around Mick's cockhead, and when he did, Mick growled for him. The sound was full of pride, and he hummed, letting Mick feel the vibrations.

"I'm going to fuck you into the middle of next week, baby," Mick said, stroking his cheeks.

Promise? He wanted it. He wanted to feel Mick's cock all the way in the back of his throat.

"Mmmm." Mick started to rock, not seeming to be worried at all about choking him. In this, Mick clearly thought he could hold his own.

He relaxed his throat and trusted, knowing in his soul that Mick had him, that Mick believed in him.

Those rough hands caught in his hair, and Mick panted, rocking, pushing him, and he grabbed that tight, muscular ass to have something to hold onto. If Mick came from this, would there be a round three?

"Not going to shoot. I want your ass. I want to feel you come around my cock."

He jerked. Had Mick read his mind? Maybe he was just

that obvious. He was sucking cock and humping the bed, after all.

He didn't care. Whatever it was, he was here with his mate. He was going to take it.

"That's it, baby. Take it all in. Then I'll fuck that hot ass of yours. I dream about that and wake up in a cold sweat."

God, the things Mick was saying to him. Kit had never even had a dream this good, so he knew he wasn't just asleep or unconscious.

He nodded, bouncing his lips down over Mick's cock. He wanted it. All of it. So he sucked hard all the way up and dared to push Mick's balls up against the base of his cock.

Kit would swear he felt the blast of Mick's pleasure in his brain before Mick filled his mouth with hot seed.

He swallowed convulsively, trying desperately to take it all, every drop. He needed to know this.

"Oh, baby. That was stunning." Mick finally pulled free, leaving his lips with a wet pop. Mick sank down on the bed next to him, then kissed him so hard his ears rang. Tasting him.

Tasting them. Together.

Mick covered him, resting against him and making him whimper as his cock made a comeback.

"I got you, baby. I got you." Mick nibbled his neck, then his collarbone. The bites weren't tiny, and they held promises of teeth and bruises. Kit was over the moon. He wanted Mick to mark him. To claim him.

When Mick's teeth sank into his shoulder, he cried out, his need overwhelming.

Mine.

Yes! Yes, every bit! Look at that. He could hear someone in his head.

He held Mick where he was, neither of them fighting this need, finally.

Mick's cock was still hard, prodding at his thigh, and Kit wanted to feel it inside him. He wanted to have the stretch, the burn.

"Soon. Soon, Kit."

"Uh-huh. Soon. I got stuff—for tugging off." They would need it. The goo, which he'd forgotten the word for. He wanted Mick to fuck him so deep he couldn't see.

"Lube, I hope. Spit isn't great for the first time. I need you slick."

His cock danced at the words, making Kit squirm. If he'd fallen and hit his head, he didn't want to wake up. "Uh-huh."

"Get it, Kit."

Like it was an alpha command, it moved him before he thought, and he reached up, digging the little bottle out. He handed it to Mick, who gave him another "better to eat you with" grin and popped the top. "This is going to be a little cold."

Mick squirted out lube, then coated his fingers. Before he could blink, Mick was pushing at his hole with one.

He started to tense, but this was Mick, his mate, and Kit knew it. He knew like he knew his bear. So he breathed deep, trying to relax so Mick could take him, could bring them together.

"Good bear. I'm going to mark you so deep you'll always know me."

Was that supposed to scare him? "Bring it on."

"Mmm. My bear." Mick was a true alpha like this, owning him, that finger sliding past the ring of muscles that tried to push him back out, teasing Kit's nerves. "So fucking tight, baby. I am going to open you up."

Kit groaned, driving down on Mick's finger, making sure Mick understood how much Kit needed this. He had ached for Mick for years, and now it was real.

"So hot, baby. So good. I can't wait to get inside you."

Mick was patient, if not slow, though, making sure his muscles relaxed before sliding another finger in.

Kit found one of the dusky nipples on Mick's chest and pinched it, rolled it like he would do his own, hoping it felt good.

The look Mick gave him almost burned him to the ground, and he got another of those searing kisses. Another finger joined the first inside him, making him grunt. He pinched harder, diving into the kiss, making Mick fight for it.

Mick bit his lower lip, which derailed his whole brain. The sting was the most perfect thing ever.

Mick's gold eyes were fastened to his, and his brain was filled with a desperate rushing thought.

Mate. Mate. Mate. Mate. Matematematematemate.

Kit spread wider. "Now. Mick."

"Just a little more." Mick stretched him, got him wet, until he thought he would scream.

"Now."

Mick growled softly, and he almost shot from the vibrations. "When I say."

"Alpha..." He was a bear, but Mick was his alpha, and the leader of their weird pack. There was no doubt of that.

And when he said it, acknowledged it, his Mick's eyes flared, the gold shining and clear.

He felt the jolt of it all the way to his toes. Then those fingers were pulling free, and Mick's cock was invading him, taking him by storm.

Kit sucked in a deep breath, his eyes rolling as his body accepted the burning log that pressed deep inside.

Mick felt huge. Superheated. Perfect. Kit held still so he could adjust, but soon he would have to move. He raised his legs to wrap them around Mick's thighs, wanting to keep them pressed together tight. He could become addicted to this.

He hummed, his eyes rolling back in his head. "Don't stop."

"No, baby. Not stopping now. Not ever." Mick slid deep inside him, hips rocking against his with these tiny movements. They were just right and not enough.

"Not ever." He pushed up, driving himself down on Mick's cock as their lips met again.

"Mmm." Mick kissed him like there was no tomorrow, though Kit might die if there wasn't one.

No dying. Just breathe and let me love you.

A sharp longing went through him. Love him. God.

Love me. Yes. Yes, please. He wasn't going to deny the possibility of this. No way.

Yes. Mick started driving into him, slamming against him, and that was what Kit needed, what he craved. Their scents mingled, rising on the air, musk heavy between them.

The world faded away, leaving nothing but them—their growls, their heat, the feeling of Mick's teeth on his skin.

Kit held on, fingers digging into Mick's shoulders. He felt taken inside and out, possessed. Mick was his mate. He knew it.

Mick's teeth drew blood, claiming him, marking him, and there was nothing on earth Kit wanted more.

Kit. Hang on, baby. Hang on tight.

Mate. Yes. I'm right here.

Mick gritted his teeth, his body moving fast, sweat dripping off his skin. Kit could see the wolf in Mick's eyes, could feel how Mick's cock swelled in him.

Kit grabbed his own cock, pulling hard, wanting to get off with his Mick.

"That's it, baby. Come on. You can do it. M'close. So close." Mick's eyelids fluttered, but he kept those amazing eyes open.

His body clamped down, and Mick howled, their orgasms crashing, one after another.

Mick's heat inside him made his poor balls empty everything he had left, which he hadn't thought was a lot. He came until he actually ached.

He closed his eyes, the bed seeming like it was still moving, still spinning in lazy circles.

"Shhh." Mick stroked his hair back off his forehead. "Rest, Kit. Just rest. I'll be right here."

"Promise?"

"I promise. Even if the guys call. I won't go without bringing you with me." Mick kissed his closed eyelids, still inside him.

"I love you." He knew it was stupid to say, but he meant it.

"I love you, too, baby. Never doubt that for a minute."

He believed it. He just didn't know if Mick meant it the same way he did.

It didn't matter. All the adrenaline of the day caught up with him, and Kit was asleep in minutes. He only had time to hope he didn't bear out in his sleep and crush Mick before he was out.

———

Mick woke up on top of Kit, feeling sore and a little crusty, but otherwise amazing.

He'd wanted to do that for ages.

Knowing he was Kit's first time did make him feel a little guilty. Not because of what they'd done. But because he'd thought he would be gentle if Kit was a virgin. Sweet.

Instead, he'd gone all alpha and taken Kit like they were the last two men on earth.

He wasn't sorry. God fucking knew, he would do the same thing again. But he did feel a little like a dick.

Kit was dreaming, the hum in the back of his head total satisfaction. His bear was happy. The song still had a lot of mate in it, but Mick wasn't worried by that.

He agreed.

They had a lot of baggage to work through. He knew that. It didn't matter. They would.

As long as he could keep Kit from running off.

He hadn't realized how close he'd come to losing his bear, how he'd caused unintentional hurt to the most important man in his life. His team meant so much to him. They were his family. But he loved Kit with everything in him.

Maybe he had no idea how to treat Kit most of the time, because every protective instinct surged in him and he always wanted to give Kit the safe stuff to do so he would stay in one piece.

Now he knew that he had caused harm instead of preventing it. Dammit.

His phone buzzed in his pants on the floor.

Mick scooted to the edge of the bed, relieved he and Kit weren't glued together, though a shower would be good. "Hartness."

"Boss. Need you at the command center. Can you come on up?" James was all business.

"Kit and I will be there in less than twenty." He needed clean clothes and a spit bath, and so did Kit. Whatever it was, James wasn't coding it a 911.

"Good deal. See you in twenty." The phone went dead.

Kit groaned and shook his head, trying to wake himself up. "What's wrong?"

"James must have something. They want to see us upstairs. We don't have time for a shower, but come on and let's get cleaned up and change." That way Kit knew they were a united front. A them.

"Yeah. Yeah. You want a shirt?" Kit sat up, running his

fingers through his thick black hair. Mick's bruise was right there on his shoulder.

"We'll clean up here, then stop by mine so I can get some clothes." That would waste the least time.

"Sounds good." Kit dragged him to the bathroom, then started the shower. "It will take us two minutes without shampooing and is way easier than a washcloth." The steam came out right away, and he was glad he'd put in those tankless water heaters.

Kit grabbed two towels, and he stepped in, rinsing himself off. Kit used Irish Spring, and the smell made his nostrils tingle. He loved that scent, and now he knew why. When Kit popped in, too, Mick scrubbed him really fast. They didn't have time to get busy. The team needed them.

Still, he was going to touch every time he got the opportunity to, dammit.

Kit chuckled when Mick scrubbed his pits. "Tickles, you jerk."

"Too damn bad." He reached around to pinch that amazing ass, then rinsed them off. They needed to move. Damn it.

Mick had this puppy urge to play. That was the result of the amazing sex.

At some point, he intended to be able to take Kit somewhere, woo him, spend time with him. Have fun. Everyone else had gotten a honeymoon period to solidify the mate bond. Soon. Soon it would be their turn.

They dried off, Kit dressed, and Mick wore one of Kit's shirts to his place so he could get clothes on as well.

He brought Kit into his apartment, partially because he didn't want Kit out of his sight, and partially because he needed Kit's scent in his place.

"You are a slob, Mick."

"Like you didn't know that." His stress levels showed in

his space. Right now, he was stressed as fuck, so his apartment looked like a bomb had gone off. He did have clean clothes though. He slipped into a pair of workout pants and a long-sleeved tee. "Ready?"

"I am. Let's get upstairs and see what James found out." Kit stood by the door, holding it open for him as they headed out.

"Yeah. I hope it's good."

Kit snorted wryly. Yeah. They could use some good news, but at this point, they didn't believe in it.

There wasn't anything good left in this nightmare of a situation, but they were going to get ahead of it if it killed him.

They headed into the tech office, where James greeted them by rolling over in his office chair to hand him a sheaf of printouts. "Coroner ruled cause of death as drug overdose. We have some video from the prison."

"Did you see the shape-shifter or Maldinado?" Kit asked, his bear vibrating.

"I think you'll be interested to see this, bear."

The video when Patel had broken out showed them nothing. This one...just as the guard left the cell with Hetrick, there was a flicker of something. Hetrick slammed the guard into the doorframe, and his face blurred, his eyes glowing with animal shine like a dog who'd been caught by a camera flash.

"Shit. So he's really a shape-shifter."

Rey snorted. "Anyone else having an X-Men moment?"

Everyone stared but Kit, who chuckled. "Mystique was way hotter than this guy."

James rolled his eyes. "Nerds."

"You're just jealous." Kit stuck his tongue out at James, and Mick chuckled. It felt good, seeing Kit play.

They all needed that. Downtime had been hard to catch.

"Okay, so how do we get rid of a guy like that? Or get him out from under Maldinado's control?" Mick asked.

"I contacted some people back home." Brock sighed softly and shook his head. "He wanted to know all sorts of things we don't know, but he was pretty sure he could help us."

"Can he come here?" Kit asked.

Brock snorted. "He never leaves the rainforest. But he has the technology to look at the video. I will send it to him, and he will help us."

"So your friend that doesn't leave the rainforest has...Wi-Fi?" Rey blinked at him.

"Dial-up."

"Wow." James threw his hands up.

"Hey, if he knows what these...thingies are, we should be glad," Grizz snapped.

"I can still judge his internet speed."

Kit chuckled softly. "We are geeks, after all, right, guys?"

Rey hooted. "You know it, buddy. Nerds to the core!"

Mick shook his head. "I am way too manly for that."

"Says the man who owns every episode and movie with the original Star Trek cast, as well as a bunch of vintage merch," Kit teased.

"Shut up, you." Mick chuffed softly, pleased. He'd been sure Kit would be shy and distant with him.

Grizz hooted. "Now the truth comes out."

Hank came in with a tray of coffee drinks and a bag of some kind of pastry. "What did I miss?"

"Mick's Star Trek obsession," Grizz said. "You might be the only not geek."

Hank snorted. "Shit, man. Have you seen my Lord of the Rings collection? I got it all out of storage."

"Really?" Mick blinked. "Elves?"

"Elves. Orcs. Dwarves. Hobbits. Ents. If it's Tolkien, I'm in."

Brock sighed. "You have all lost the thread."

"Send your man the stuff, Brock. It can't be any worse

than fumbling around in the dark like we are now. And if he's in on it with Maldinado, well, then the man will know we're onto him." Mick pressed a hand to James's shoulder. "Anything else?"

"Yeah." James called up a report. "Two cops at your buddy Greg's office went to the hospital this morning with what they thought was food poisoning, but they still haven't figured out what's wrong. Rey's source says neither is a cat shifter, but one is a wolf and one is a coyote."

"Shit. I'll call him." Greg should have called him, damn it. What was going on?

"Don't bother. No one knows where he is."

"What?"

James shrugged. "The entire department's in an uproar. He's gone."

"Gone?" He blinked.

"I'll get on the horn with Cole," Hank said.

"Now," Mick barked.

"Don't snarl. I'm on it." Hank bared his teeth, already pulling out his phone.

He would have apologized, but Hank didn't need it. He knew that.

Kit came to grab his hand. "He'll be okay."

"I know he will." Except he didn't. Greg had been planning to do something insane, and he knew it. The man had managed to go undercover, just like he'd said he would, but was he safe, or had Maldinado's people known who he was all along?"

"Uh-huh. Okay. Keep me posted. Yeah. I'll look out for it." Hank hung up. "Cole is sending me a burn phone to call on from now on. He says Greg checked in ten hours ago and he was alive and well, if not safe in that organization."

"Where are you picking it up?"

"I'm meeting one of Cole's people at a King Sooper."

"No." Kit shook his head. "No, we know they're drugging felines and lupines. Tell him I'll meet him. I'm safe-ish."

"I'll go with you and be your getaway," Mick said. He knew his tone brooked no arguments, but he would let Kit make the pickup without him. He would trust the universe.

Kit nodded. "That's the most logical. They'll know Grizz. No one knows me."

Brock chewed his lip. "I hate it, but he's right."

"Then that's how we do it." Mick sighed. "I'll go as incognito as I can, but I can't promise to stay too far away. I want to be there if you get in the shit."

"I've got this." *But I'm glad you'll be there.*

I know you do. No one goes out alone though. Mick wasn't letting anyone get taken or injured if he could help it.

That's fair. Kit stared at him. *I can hear you. I really hear you inside me.*

Get used to it, buster. He grinned, and Kit laughed, and damn if everyone didn't look at them and raise eyebrows.

No one said a word, even though Rey was bouncing in his chair like he was about to explode.

"Stop it," Mick said. "Tell us where, Hank."

His phone dinged. "I forwarded you the text."

"Thanks. Let's go, Kit." He wanted his bear armed and prepared and ready for any situation.

"Yes, boss."

They headed out to get that burn phone so Greg would have a whole other level of protection. No one should be in the wind.

———

Kit was scared, and he wouldn't admit it. Not to Mick. Not to the others. Shit, not even to himself.

All he had to do was go into the store, get the phone, and

walk out. No sweat. And dammit, he was going to act like it was no sweat.

But this was the first time he hadn't been berserker-raging in danger. The first time he wasn't a virgin.

The first time he had a mate.

He took a deep breath, then let his shoulders slump and his chin dip. Not because he was ashamed, but because he knew it would make him look...doughier. Less intimidating. He was a big guy, and people could get squirrely.

There's nothing doughy about you, baby. You're built like a brick shit house.

His cheeks heated. *Distracting me.* But it felt fine, so fine, to hear.

Mmhmm. Are you sore?

No. I can feel you. I want to feel you again.

Good. I want you to. Mick wasn't letting Kit's nerves get the better of him one bit. He was just keeping Kit that little bit off-balance, but that would let him be alert, which he appreciated.

His mate was a butthead. The most beautiful, studly, amazing butthead on earth.

He stepped up to the counter at the store. "I have a pickup for Henry." No one ever called Hank *Henry*. Ever.

"Let me look." The lady took her time, searching the bags sort of one at a time.

God, it was taking forever.

He didn't fidget. He did pull out his phone and act like the bored twenty-something everyone saw when they looked at him. If you were what people expected to see, they never looked again.

Kit figured he had learned from the best—no matter which of the team he picked, they were the very best.

"Found it. Here you go."

"Thank you." He took the package from her, nodded, and headed for the door, checking his six as casually as he could.

The walk across the dark parking lot seemed like miles.

He got back in the POS sedan with Mick, and he let out his breath in a rush. "Let me check the bag." He needed to scour it for devices or residue before they took it back to the office. He found nothing, so he let Mick look, too, just in case. They even tore open the package and looked the phone over really well.

"Looks good, baby. Let's head back so James can set it up. I worry about Greg, and we can't just leave him to the Feds."

"Sounds good to me." He wanted, so badly, to ask if he'd done okay, but he didn't want to seem unconfident.

Mick turned to look him right in the eye. "That was a good job, Kit. You blended right in." He could feel it in his mind that Mick wasn't humoring him. He'd done well, and Mick was giving him his due.

It was the best thing he'd ever heard.

"Thanks. I went for dorky young adult with a phone addiction." As opposed to dorky well-trained bear with a wolf addiction.

Mick chuckled, getting the car going.

Kit thought neither of them took an easy breath until they got back to the office, the car parked in the big underground garage, the doors locked behind them.

"You're all clear." Rey's voice filled the car through the radio. "Doors are locked. No tails."

"Thanks, buddy." Kit looked over at Mick. "We did it."

"We did." Mick gave him a hard kiss across the console. "Can you take that up to Hank and James? I want to make some calls. I'll be in my office."

He was a little dingy from the kiss for a second, a bit breathless, but he nodded. "On it."

"Thanks, baby. I'll be out in half an hour or so to check in."

"No worries. I've got this." Kit nodded and slipped out of the car, taking the phone up to the kitties on the third floor.

"Hey, thanks, man. Good job."

"You had eyes?" That shouldn't surprise him. James saw all.

"He hacked the store's camera," Rey said. "I need a snack and to unbend my neck a minute. Want to come to the lounge with me?" Rey's gyrating eyebrows told Kit he wanted to talk.

"Yeah. Totally. Dr Pepper and Cheetos?" He knew what Rey liked.

"Heck, yeah. And oatmeal raisin cookies."

"I'm in."

They made their way toward the stairs, all of them having learned the elevator was only to be used sparingly. Just in case. They were about halfway down when something sounded like it hit the outside of the building like a two-ton truck, and the stairs shook under them.

"Get upstairs with James and get us eyes!" He started hurtling down the stairs, his bear coming right to the surface.

He growled, needing to protect his team. Kit was flashing back to a whole flotilla of croc shifters taking out the very foundation of the goddamn building. He would not allow that to happen again.

"What the fuck?" Mick howled, and he knew his lover was on the way to join him.

"Hurry! Grizz, I need you!" Another bear would have the size advantage with him, and he thought they'd need that.

Grizz and Brock met them at the landing.

"No cats!" Mick growled, waving Brock off.

"Fuck that. I need—"

"Brock! Someone needs to help upstairs. Please. They've

only got Dylan to protect them." Kit needed Brock to understand. Brock would defend the others.

Brock snarled, but he whirled and sprinted upstairs, Locke keeping in step with him. They needed to be the front line, the three of them. The alpha and his bears.

Another, smaller tremor hit the building, and Kit roared. This was their home, they needed to settle this.

"It's an explosive device. The secondary just blew. Doors are holding." James sounded so solid, so calm.

"Goddamn it."

"Be careful. I electrified the inner door. Take the small side entrance out."

"Do you see anyone out there?" Grizz asked.

"No." James sounded sure.

Rey cleared his throat. "Looks like the explosive was on a drone. You closed the door on it when you came in."

"Shit. So much for no tail." Kit was furious. They'd almost brought in a bomb. "A fucking drone."

Mick growled but stopped them before they went outside. "Rooftop report, James."

"Clear for a quarter of a mile as far as I can see. You know how CCTV is."

"Yeah. It sucks." Kit and Grizz stood at the side door, and he put his paw on the handle. "Ready, Grizz?"

"Ready, Kit. Whatever you find that's live, get it away."

"Will do." His muzzle was growing, his clothes tearing, and Mick let them loose, two bears galloping out into the street. They were protecting their mates.

They destroyed the remains of explosives, batting the final two small flashbangs away with harsh, vicious blows.

Kit lifted his nose to the air, ignoring the acrid scent of the bomb. He wanted to see if there was an unfamiliar human or animal scent around the building. He saw Grizz do the same.

They caught the scent at the exact same time, and they gave chase, galloping across the parking lot.

A motorcycle revved, then peeled out, the man on it compact and well-balanced, but completely unfamiliar. Another of Maldinado's hired hands?

Come back, love. You're wearing yourselves out. I don't want you caught out there.

As if Grizz could hear Mick, too, he slowed, then stopped, head hanging as he panted. Bears could chase fast, but not for very long.

Grizz headbutted him, and they started back in, moving slower, their bodies betraying them.

Mick met them, still in his human body, already on the phone. "Yeah, Pope. I need you to come look at the bay door. No. Bomb. Yeah, tell me about it. Thanks, man. Be careful."

Pope was the engineering genius who'd fortified their new building.

"In." Mick pushed them both back in the door, locking it behind them.

Kit reached for his human self, but it was fighting the exhaustion, and he flopped down to rest a moment. Mick brought him and Grizz water to help perk them back up.

Dylan came in with blankets, covering them, and they rested hard, panting as they fought to gather energy.

"Brock is waiting upstairs just in case. He says he's going to kick your furry ass for running amok," Dylan said.

Grizz snorted, the sound so human from such a big bear.

"Our berserker bears." Mick's voice was filled with sarcasm.

He lifted his head and curled his lip. *We got a lead for James. Flushed out the motorcycle guy.*

He could have shot you.

A guy on a bike with a drone? No way. He's a techie killer, not a hands-on guy.

Mate, I will bite you and make you cry.

Not like this you won't. The idea of Mick's bite was lovely, though, and the sound of 'mate' in his voice was perfect.

Grrr.

Kit took a deep breath, and his body finally listened, and it shrank under the blanket, his human form emerging. He poked Locke. "Come on, Grizz. Brock needs to see you and we need food and juice."

Grizz slowly morphed, the blanket seeming to deflate. "Juice."

"Yeah. I'll pour you both some apple if you drag your asses upstairs," Mick said. "Good work, boys, even if you took ten years off my life."

"Fussy old wolf," Kit teased.

"Older every day."

They crept upstairs, Brock meeting them halfway, the Portuguese flying hard and fast.

Grizz just chuckled. "Shh. I'm fine. He didn't really want to kill anyone. If we can catch him, I bet we can turn him on Maldinado. Better than him ending up dead."

Kit wasn't sure about that, but he wasn't going to argue. He wanted his juice and a bite.

Mick poured juice at the lounge, and Rey brought him and Grizz sweats.

"So, James. Did you get anything on the guy?"

"I ran facial recognition, and it's the dead prison guard. So that was our shifter."

"No shit? Damn it." Kit hated being wrong. He would have said Grizz was right and that he wasn't a hands-on killer. "Then we need to take his ass down. I can try to follow him."

Surely there would be a scent trail that he could follow, if he could shift again so soon.

"Stop it. I'm doing my best to follow the CCTV trail, and to keep an eye out for that bike." James poked Kit's arm. "In fact. I'm going back to work. I just wanted to check on you guys." He turned and headed out. Hank hadn't come with, so he must be manning the monitors.

Kit opened his mouth to argue, and Mick popped a donut hole in his gob to shut him up.

He almost choked, but it tasted too good to waste, so he chewed it.

"I like that, boss." James chuckled and shook his head. "I like my fingers, though, so I'll let you do it."

"He's mostly tame." The heated look Mick gave him took the sting out of it.

"Grr." He opened his mouth for another bite.

Mick fed him another donut hole, then gave Locke one too. Not that the look was the same at all.

He might have almost growled.

"He needs his strength, baby. I'll turn him over to Brock ASAP."

His money was actually on Brock, when he thought about it, but whatever. Mick was his.

Grizz chuckled. "Okay. I'm going to my apartment. Holler if you need me. I know James and Rey are on this guy."

Brock was back from wherever he'd gone, arm sliding around Grizz. Ah, he also had a big bag of food from the kitchen.

Kit sat there, wishing that he could have chased the shapeshifter down.

They were alone suddenly, and Mick fed him another donut before eating one himself.

"Thanks." He managed the word between chews.

"Mmm. These are good. You scared me. But you guys did good."

"We're the least vulnerable, right?" They were solid as rocks.

"I know. But that doesn't mean he can't get you. Maldinado has been crazy good at hurting us." Mick sighed, then ate more donuts. "Let me eat my feelings some."

"Fair enough." Like he cared. He really didn't. Mick could eat whatever he wanted, and he'd be happy.

Mick scooted a chair close to him, leaning on him, and that was even better than just watching Mick eat. The warm weight of Mick against him, the trust Mick showed, amazed him.

"Hey." He leaned in, panting softly. "I'm sorry I didn't catch him. He was just too fast out of the gate or I would have torn the tires off that bike with my teeth."

"I'm not sure I'm sorry. I'm glad you didn't get too close. He's a shape-shifter. If he'd shifted into you or Locke…"

"You would know." He met Mick's eyes. *You would know, mate. You would know he wasn't me.*

I would, but that would still send me into a rage, him wearing your face. Mick reached up to touch his cheek. "We need to catch this guy. He can't be allowed to keep doing this shit for Maldinado or anyone else."

"No shit." Kit wanted normalcy back. He wanted to be able to—he didn't know, have a real life. He was just getting on par with his peers, getting Mick's respect and need and love. How much could they explore if it wasn't one emergency after another?

"We'll do it. The fortifications held. That's a huge turning of the tide. We're not really even limping from it. I mean, I know he was just testing, but still, this is a good thing." Mick stood. "We're regrouping. Come have a shower."

"Yeah? Like with you again?" He wasn't sure he could get it up, but he wanted to try if it meant being naked and alone with Mick. Who was his lover.

"Yeah. You had a hell of an adrenaline rush shifting. You'll be sore. I can help." Mick waggled his eyebrows.

His cock stirred. Go him. Looked like he could go for it,

indeed. He took Mick's hand and let his mate pull him to his feet. He was pretty sore and sweaty and worn to the bone.

He could so use a rubdown. From Mick. All over.

Four

Mick sat with his back to the pillows up against the headboards and scrolled through his emails. Kit's even breathing told him his lover was still asleep, which was good. The kind of crazy shift-and-run Kit and Locke had done could really take it out of a guy.

He'd messaged James for information and gotten, "Working on it", so he'd decided to just catch up on admin work. Since Carrie had quit, Mick had been reluctant to take on another admin right now and put someone else in danger, so they were all DIYing their scut work.

He scrolled, deleting the bacon and spam, answering a billing question.

Kit frowned, hands sliding on the sheets, and he patted Kit's back, murmuring love words. Might as well let him sleep while he could. If Maldinado was ramping up again, it would start coming in waves.

He clicked on an email from the web form, one that said he was just going to give a quote, and he scowled at what popped up.

We're coming for you, puppy.

The image was one of a bear's paws, sawed off at the wrists.

"Jesus." He kept his voice down, but that was shocking, and his whole body tensed up. Fucker.

He sent it to James with *a track this message*.

The next message didn't have words—it was a disemboweled jaguar.

"Goddamn it!"

Kit popped up, his eyes going wide. "What?"

"Someone is sending me threats over email. From the web form. Christ on a cracker."

"Send it to James?"

He closed the email. He wasn't showing this filth to his mate. "I did. With a warning. That was horrendous." He saw a lot of shit in his job, but when someone went to all that trouble to make it relate to people he loved, it turned Mick's stomach.

"I'm sorry. That bastard hates Brock, bad, doesn't he?"

"Insanely. I mean, this isn't just your average ex, honey. This is a murderous obsession." Maldinado was going to pick them off one by one, too, if he could. Like cutting off Brock's limbs.

"Well, Brock is ours. Our pack. Our family. He's evil, but we have love."

"We do. And we've survived everything he's tossed at us." Mick chuckled. "He must be pretty frustrated, in fact."

"I bet. I can't understand hurting someone you, love. I just want to feed you and touch you and spend time with you."

"Yeah. It's a twisted mind that does that. I'm glad he has Locke." Then Mick registered what Kit had said, and he grinned. "And I want you to do all that too. Also, I always want your ass."

"Pervert." Kit blushed and chuckled, then pressed their lips together.

Kit didn't want to be treated like a kid, so Mick was following orders. And he loved that he was a bit of a perv. In fact, he had some very bad things he wanted to do with Kit as they bonded. That big body fascinated him.

It's yours. You're the only one that's had me. Ever.

I can't even with that, love. It makes me nuts. Makes me hard. He'd given Kit a hand in the shower, but he could stand an orgasm now. Or two.

Good. I'm yours. All yours. Kit slowly put the computer aside, and Mick hid his smile. So daring.

His Kit had waited long enough for his attention, he guessed. Now Kit was going to go for what he wanted, damn the torpedoes, full speed ahead. Mick could admire that.

"You want something, baby?"

"I do." Kit's dark eyes were lit from within. "I want to taste you. Is it okay?"

"That is so okay you don't even know. I want you." His cock was already rising just from him thinking about it. Kit inspired him.

"I want to taste you again. Seriously. I need to." Kit wandered down his chest, licking and tasting him, lapping one nipple almost lazily.

He sank a hand into Kit's shaggy hair and tugged, not wanting him to linger too long. Things were getting urgent below the waist already.

Kit growled softly, nipping him. Little shit.

"Don't make me bite back, baby. I do it harder," Mick warned.

That little shiver proved that Kit wasn't all that worried or put off by the threat.

Maybe he even thought that would feel good.

Mick grinned, feeling a little feral.

He'd never dared believe that his sweet bear had so much need. Now he knew, though, and he couldn't wait to explore.

"Lower, Kit. I need your mouth."

"I'm working on it."

"Work faster," he ordered. Mick knew damn well Kit would do what he wanted, but he could encourage, couldn't he?

"You're pushing." Kit's laughter tickled his belly, all the way down.

"I am. I need it. I'm hungry for you, baby. Want to feel you, know you're safe and here and mine." He rubbed Kit's shoulders.

"I'm here and yours." Kit's chin nudged the tip of his prick, just a little hard.

Stubbly. Damn. Mick grunted. "Oh, fuck. Do that again."

Kit swung that huge head the barest bit, side to side. It felt like being stroked with a feather, then a bit of sandpaper. Over and over.

Then, about the time he was going to scream, Kit's lips wrapped around his cockhead.

The wet heat was soothing to his abused skin, and then it wasn't. The sting was maddening, and then there was suction and friction. Kit loved on him like no one else had, ever.

Kit glanced up at him as if he'd heard, eyes wide.

Mick smiled, tracing Kit's stretched lips. "It's the truth."

Love. The simple word rocked him, the truth of it stunning.

Yes. Love. He meant it. Kit was...well, his mate. Once in a lifetime, even lives as long as theirs. Mick had denied it as long as he could to let Kit grow up, but he couldn't, wouldn't, push it aside anymore.

They had a lot to learn about each other for two people who knew each other as well as they did.

Kit worked him, the suction clumsy but hungry, demanding.

He rolled with it, pushing up but not too hard. No choking his lover. That could lead to a toothy disaster.

Kit groaned, the sound vibrating around his cock.

"Love how you feel. Love how much you want me." He had to admit, that was a hell of a loop of pleasure they had going, mind to mind. Somehow they were spinning together, flying.

He hadn't known this was possible, to feel so much.

Mick. Mate. You make me soar.

I want to make you roar. The image of a flying bear did make him chuckle though. He thought Kit might have gotten it, too, because he snorted.

"No laughing with my cock in your mouth, Kit."

Kit rolled his eyes and slapped his shaft with the flat of his tongue.

"That's it. Only sucking and licking and—uhn."

Kit had pushed down as far as he could go, lips sealed tight, and damn. Damn.

Such a good bear. Fuck him raw. He let his hips roll, just the slightest bit, taking Kit's lips.

He wanted to be good and hard and wet when he pulled out and went after Kit's ass. Which he would. He had to. This was amazing, but not how he wanted to come.

Kit's mental voice sang to him, and he loved it, how Kit loved his flavor. He petted and stroked and waited as long as he could.

Then he had to pull free, laughing when Kit grumbled. "I want to fuck you, baby. Bad. Now."

"Oh. Yeah?" Kit leaned down and kissed the tip of his prick.

"Yeah. I want in you. Grab the lube." He was wet, but not enough. Kit needed some stretching. He wouldn't hurt his mate. Period. And his bear had been through a lot in a very few hours.

Especially his ass.

"Lube," Kit said, grabbing it, then dropping it into Mick's hand.

"So efficient. I should make you get yourself ready." Kit swayed, pupils blown, and Mick handed the lube back. "Do it, baby."

"Mean to me." Kit slicked his fingers and slipped them behind himself. That wasn't right. Mick couldn't see.

"Turn so I can see you, baby. Put on a show for me." He slapped the flat of his hand against that bouncing cock, which was so damn pretty. Mick wasn't opposed to catching once in a while. He'd have to ride that sometime soon.

He bet it would feel like taking a club.

Kit shook a little, breath coming hard as he swiveled so Mick could see him. "Oh. That was deep."

"Gotta watch that. Was it good?"

"Uh-huh."

"It looked like it."

Kit blushed a deep, dark red, but his bear didn't look away, didn't hide a bit, letting him in to see all that passion.

He couldn't tear his gaze away. Kit was a work of art.

"I'm ready for you. I am."

"Let me feel." He circled that sweet hole with his finger, testing.

"Feel deeper. I need you."

"Soon, baby. Soon." He pushed that finger in, letting Kit feel it. He quirked his finger, dragging along the soft insides.

Kit danced for him, belly pulling in, cock bobbing. "Please."

"There, hmm?" Mick chuckled and stroked again and again.

"No. No, I need you. Your dick. God, Mick. Please. I need you in me. Take me."

He felt so tall, so important, so incredibly needed.

He took a deep breath and pulled his finger and Kit's free, then grabbed Kit by the hips to guide him up and let him ride.

"Need you." Kit sank down on his prick, taking him in, inch by inch, that heat wrapping around him.

"That's it, baby. Right there. Come on." He moaned when Kit hit bottom, ass on his thighs. He tilted Kit's hips, cock dragging along those tight muscles.

"Mmm." Kit stretched up long, eyes heavy lidded, lips parted. "Finally."

"Greedy bear." He loved it. He'd never felt so wanted.

"With you." Kit panted, trying to move, but Mick held him down. The leverage was still mostly his so far.

"Stay. I want you to feel me. Every inch of me."

"I will. I just..." Kit wiggled a little, then stilled. "There. Oh."

"Yeah. Right fucking there, baby." He wanted to howl with how good it was.

Kit nodded, throat working hard enough that Mick could see it.

"Come on, baby. Now it's time to move." He grabbed Kit's cock like a handle, ready to help him move.

"Thank goodness." Kit's eyes rolled and his bear grabbed the headboard, driving down onto his cock like a wild thing.

He grunted, his eyes rolling back into his head. Jesus, Kit could take a pounding, and it was heated and sweaty and perfect. Mick would remember this his whole life if he only got now, but he was praying for forever. He just had to keep his family, his pack, safe. Especially his mate.

"Stop thinking. Fuck me." Kit's growl tore through him.

"I am! Trust me, baby. I am right here with you."

"And I've never been safer. I want you. I want you to touch me and fucking love me."

He growled, tugging Kit's dick. "I do love you, damn it."

"Good. I need it. More than anything." Kit rolled forward, then slammed back.

"Uhn!" He lost words, his cock in that tight grasp, Kit clamping down around it. His mouth went dry, and he fought to find the perfect rhythm to drive them both insane.

Not that it took much. Kit was moaning continuously, his skin flushed, his muscles tight. Nothing on earth was more beautiful. Not one damn thing. Not even a steak with peanut butter sauce. Or maple bacon.

Nothing. This sight was necessary, and he would do anything to keep it.

"That kind of thinking I like." Kit bounced, his skin damp, his cock slapping his belly.

He reached up, tweaking Kit's nipple hard, just as a distraction.

"Mick! Fuck. Stop. I can't—I'm gonna die."

"Nope. No dying. I know you can do this. I want to feel you come around me."

Kit groaned and nodded but couldn't manage any words at all, just that hot body squeezing around him.

Mick chuffed, his need going up another level from where he already was. Lord, he was gonna blow any second. His breath heaved in his chest, his vision clouding.

Kit clenched around him, milking his cock like that hole was a fist.

Mick shouted, unable to hold back anymore, and he came hard, his breath whooshing right out of his body. "Kit!"

Kit followed along right behind him, ropes of spunk spraying from him. That big body came down like a felled tree, and Mick was glad he wasn't easily squashed. It felt amazing, actually.

He held Kit with all his might, not wanting to let go.

"I love you." The words were soft, whispered, and well meant.

"I love you, too, baby. Rest with me. If James finds something, we might not have a chance for a bit."

"If it got this over, it would be worth it." Kit kissed him, and he had to agree. He wanted bonding time with his mate. Vacation.

"Me too. I want fuzzy time."

"Grooming. I want to take you out to a meal."

Kit chuckled. "I want to go to a movie together with popcorn."

Oh, by the moon. He and Kit would have to work to find the right movies to enjoy together.

"Then we will. Soon. We'll just have to push him to make a move."

Kit yawned, his jaw popping audibly. "We will. God, I just had a nap, and I want another one."

He patted Kit's back. "Rest. I like you where you are."

"Then I'll stay." Kit relaxed down, head on his pillows.

It was an amazing place to be.

———

Kit had showered and dressed. Mick was on some sort of conference call with the cops who worked with the guy who had disappeared undercover, so he went in search of a snack and then James and Rey. He needed to see if there was any information out there.

"Hey." James got up as soon as he walked into the tech office and came to rub noses with him. "I need your help."

"Of course." He would do anything for his team, and they knew it. "Are you going to have me do something awful?"

He knew James had a tiny wicked streak.

"Not the way you wish." James chewed his lower lip. "Grizz had to go out on assignment. He had a meet that he'd set up that he couldn't cancel. He and Brock had a huge fight because Brock wanted to go, and Grizz told him no way. Drugs. Darts. Yadda."

Kit got that. He didn't want James or Hank leaving the building either. The cats were just more vulnerable, especially to that Peaches drug. Grizz was huge and had very little reaction to tranqs, which bears could actually be sensitive to. He was a natural choice to go out.

"So..."

James sighed. "So Brock is holed up. He's got his devices turned off. I worry he's going to do something stupid."

"And you want me to go see him?" He was confused. James and Brock were super close, like brothers. "Why not you?"

"He won't talk to me. I think he thinks I read him too well. Will you check on him?"

Kit snorted. "Sometimes it's good to be harmless."

"You know it." James winked and rubbed their noses together. "Brother bear, I have seen you tear off heads. You are far from harmless. But Brock will be confident you can't stop him from doing anything."

"True." He shrugged. "Sure. I'll head down. If I'm not back, you know he Brazilian-ninja'ed me." Brock had some black-ops moves none of them were equal to.

"Fair enough. Don't let him get the drop on you."

Yeah, that was comforting. Shit.

He wandered down and headed straight to Brock's apartment, banging on the door. "Brock! It's me!"

There was nothing but silence, but James would have known if Brock had left his apartment.

"I know you're in there. I'm the least offensive one James can send. He will work his way up to Mick once the boss is off the phone, and he has a master key." He tapped his foot, hoping the threat was enough. He needed to talk the jaguar out of the tree.

"Don't make me kill you, baby bear." Brock's voice was right there by the door, and he had to fight the urge to jump.

"That would just get you in trouble too. I'm going to come in, sit for a bit, tell James you're not looking like you've got mange, and go back to the garage."

"Oh." Brock looked like hell when he opened the door, dark circles under his eyes, his face drawn, his hair in agitated clumps. "You're not going to tell me not to be stupid?"

"Of course not. You're not stupid. You're smart and tactical and really good at what you do. But this is personal, right? Like this guy wants to kill you. That has to make you nuts." He brushed past Brock into the apartment, heading for the little kitchen. He would make some tea.

"Yes. And I hate fighting with Grizz. I hate it. This is entirely my fault."

"Bullshit." Kit knew better. He believed it with all his heart. "It's not your fault Maldinado is a psychopathic fuckmonkey."

"He is. He really is." Brock sighed. "I keep debating, should I tell you guys everything? Does it matter?"

Kit paused, turning to look at Brock, wanting to pick his words carefully. "I think we know most of it. If the rest is torture porn? There's no sense in you reliving it just for some kernel of information we probably can't use. I know Hank and James and their whiteboards think everything is super important and want every detail... But I think some of your secrets can stay yours."

Brock reached for him, hand shaking. "Thank you. I— thank you."

"You know it." He took Brock's hand. The tea could wait a minute. Grizz was Brock's mate. Grizz would know the truth. The rest of them didn't need to. "Can I give you a hug? Is that weird?" It was never weird before.

"It's not weird." Brock surged up to hug him, and Kit

enfolded him, feeling Brock's almost feverish forehead against his neck.

That was one stressed-out kitty.

"It's not your fault, Brock. It's not. He chose this. He's a nutbag. You didn't ask for this."

This was like counseling victim's families, which he'd done before they locked down.

"You don't think so?"

"I know so. We are responsible for ourselves; that's it. Just our own selves."

"Mick doesn't seem to think so."

Kit scoffed. "Mick holds himself to an impossible standard, but he would never blame you for this. He's a PI. He knows what kind of shitty things regular people do to each other. Add this guy being a sociopath or psychopath or whatever to that, and no one is going to hold you responsible. No one."

Brock leaned back and searched his eyes. "You're his mate. You believe this?"

"I know it. Mick has your back. You are his pack."

Slumping, Brock seemed to wilt with relief. "I want to work with the team. I'm just so used to going it alone. And then Grizz had to leave, and I'm terrified that he'll get hurt. I couldn't stand to lose him again."

"I bet. Come spend time with us? Then we can have your back at least. That's important."

"I just—I'm not good company."

"You never are, bro." He cackled, and Brock whacked him on the shoulder. "Seriously. I'll make tater tots. We'll eat and watch TV and be catty." He grinned and waggled his eyebrows. "Did you see what I did there? Catty?"

"I did." Brock actually smiled and fist-bumped him.

"Come on. We'll eat, bitch, and groom. Make Grizz all jealous when he gets home."

"I love that." Brock slung an arm around him. "Thank you, bear."

"It's my honor." He wasn't bullshitting about that, either. He wanted to help. He needed to know he could.

"Let's go tell James I'm not crawling out a window."

"Should we invite him to come eat or no?"

"Him and Rey, yeah. Even Dylan if he's here. Mick can suck it."

That surprised a laugh out of him. Mick could indeed.

"Fair enough." He wasn't going to argue. This was about Brock. Mick would understand.

"You know I would cuddle with him if he needed it, but he needs to chew on things."

"Nom nom nom?" he teased.

"Yeah. And I'm not the thing to gnaw on."

"Nope. You're raw." He took Brock's hand to lead him out of hiding. "Tater tots. Bad TV. Grooming."

Focus was good.

Brock's laughter echoed down the hall. That was it. That was the way to make him feel part of the team. Kit got it. He'd felt like an outsider too.

Maybe they all did and that was really their common denominator.

Regardless, they were a family, a pack, and he'd never felt that so much as now.

Even if Mick could suck it.

FIVE

ick walked into the lounge after all his phone calls, about to boil over with frustration.

The sight that greeted him took a lot of the heat out of his face and the acid out of his belly.

All of his team except the big grizzly were sacked out on the couches, watching a movie through their eyelids. None of them had gotten fuzzy. That might be a bad idea right now. But they were together, resting, and not stressing.

That was a sight to behold.

He turned, ready to sneak out, and a tiny noise stopped him.

Brock was awake, beckoning to him to come sit. And there was a space between Brock and Kit...

He arched one eyebrow, and Brock nodded. Fucking A.

Mick toed off his shoes and crawled in, Kit curling into him, Brock rubbing one cheek on his shoulder, the welcome clear.

He settled in, his neck and jaw relaxing for the first time in hours. He just needed to relax some.

He could hear Kit's dreams—silly little happinesses. Honey and running, flowers and water. Him.

Mick featured hugely in Kit's dreams.

That worked for him. Kit featured in his too. He breathed deep, the smell of musk and popcorn strong in the room. The place looked like a bomb had gone off, pun intended, and he wondered how long he'd been on the phone.

And where was Grizz?

This was supposed to be a simple job—in and out. Nothing intense.

He wanted to call, but he also didn't want to alarm anyone. Grizz could get caught up talking to people. He was an old beat cop at heart, if not in practice. It was like he'd spent a long time in black ops and now he was wanting to be all out amongst them.

He refused to worry. If Grizz was in trouble, Brock would know. There was no doubt.

He would show up.

Mick closed his eyes, his hand sliding up and down Kit's back. He knew no other PI agency out there was like them. They were shifters. This kind of contact was important.

Brock's soft rumble made him sigh, his entire body relaxing into the cushion. If Brock could rest, so could he.

He woke up who knew how much later, his heart pounding. What was that? He'd heard something.

Grizz stood in the doorway of the lounge, hand up, finger to his lips. He looked a little pale, a little unsteady, and Mick would have sounded the alarm, but those eyes flashed gold, Grizz shaking his head.

So Mick slid out of the pile like a game piece out of a Jenga tower, and padded to the door as silently as he could. Grizz led the way to the front office, where the first aid kit was out.

"Thanks, boss. I need a hand, but I didn't want to freak anyone out."

"What the hell happened to you?" Now he could see that one of Locke's hands was dripping blood.

"I cut myself on broken glass. The contact I went to see had a damn shoot-out last night with some fucking drug dealer, and I've spent all this time looking for the thumb drive he was supposed to give me. I did great. Gloved up and left no trace. Cut my hand on the way out. There was glass in the door. I brought that piece of glass with me and lost my hoodie to keep the blood from dripping." Grizz rolled his eyes. "I feel like an idiot."

He snorted. "Which is why Brock didn't feel any alarm."

"Exactly. I want to shower and stuff before I go near the cats, just in case, but I need help to clean this up first."

"Let me get—"

Like a ghost, Kit appeared in the doorway with towels and a bottle of rubbing alcohol. "I smell blood."

"You do." Grizz made a face. "I'm an idiot. Cut myself on glass."

Kit tsked. "Drug guy, right? I don't smell that acrid scent of peaches."

"Good. Maybe I'll get Brock to come shower with me. I owe him an apology."

"Then let him cuddle and go join him after you bathe," Kit said. "He was feeling alone."

"You got it, cub." Grizz winked at Mick. "He's all grown."

Kit just rolled his eyes and patched Grizz up. "That's me. Grown up. I'm going to bite you, buddy."

"Seriously. You're all bossy now."

"I was bossy before. No one was listening." Kit wrapped off Locke's injury.

"Hey, we all adore you. We just needed to see you in your element like you have been."

Mick agreed. Kit had needed to be *allowed* to grow up.

He thought they had all had a less than subtle shift in attitude.

"Go clean up and then come on. I'll start another movie."

Mick grinned when Grizz was gone. "Very nice."

"Brock has been in his head too much. He needs to be with everyone, and I love Grizz, but he lets Brock wallow."

"You know everything about all of us, huh?"

"I've had a lot of chances to observe." Kit shrugged, pinking the barest bit. "You guys are my family."

"You're a good PI, Kit. You see all sorts of things." Mick took Kit's hands. "You should wash up, too, and then we'll go make food for the guys and start that movie."

"Yeah?" Kit perked up, his smile lighting up his face.

"Yeah. It's a good idea."

"Can you make poppers? I love it when you make them."

"I can." They had all the stuff. "Can you get the jalapenos out of my fridge?"

Kit had free access to his place... He had a thought about that. He would share it with Kit later.

"On it. I'll make tacos." Kit washed up, clearing everything up in that uber-organized way he had.

"Good man." They worked well together.

And they would keep on that way. They were a team.

———

Kit sent Brock and Locke off to bed with a plate of food for later, then yawned until his jaw popped. Damn. It had been a good day. Even James had set the comms to alarm if anything came up and let their engineer friend fix things while James cuddled with Hank.

Now everyone was off to cuddle more...privately.

He wandered, collecting dishes and turning off lights, and he almost jumped right out of his skin when Mick appeared in front of him. "Hey, baby. Let someone else do the rest of the dishes tomorrow. You did most of them."

"Someone else." Right. That was never going to happen. "When all this is over, we should hire a housekeeper."

"We should. I never realized Carrie did so many dishes."

"She's a total mom. She needs to find a nice he-demon and have kids." They teased that their former admin was more demon than werewolf. But she was such a neat lady.

"Well, we'll bring in a cleaning service when we're not worried they'll stab us in our sleep."

Kit grinned, but a spurt of real rage at Maldinado surprised him. "You know the only way we're going to get rid of him is to kill him and his pet shifter."

"I know. If Brock gets the chance at the kill shot, we give it to him. But any one of us will take him down if we get the chance. Heard?"

"God, yes." He would rip that bastard's head off and shit down his neck. The damage he'd done to them was immeasurable. "He's hurt us. Almost killed us. I hate him."

"I hear you, baby. We got this, though. He may be brilliant and crazy, but we're smart, a pack, and we're going to take him down."

He wanted to believe it. So he took Mick's hand when Mick held it out and believed that his lover would browbeat someone into doing dishes too.

Even if that was a stretch.

"So, staying at my place tonight, right?" Mick asked casually.

"If you want me." Hell, yes. He wanted to be with Mick, sleep with him, love him.

"I do. I was thinking. I mean..." Mick glanced at him sideways. "My place is bigger. And mostly you have electronics."

Oh.

Oh, wow. Okay.

"We could turn mine into a media room…" He held his breath, hoping he was right.

"We could. Because if we hire another admin we still have empty apartments. Shit, Rey would be over the moon to have a place to do those VR video games he likes."

Oh, damn, he was right. Hello!

His heart pounded, and he couldn't stop grinning. "I could totally move my stuff over."

"We'll bring your bed, huh? It's better for if you bear out, but I have a cooler couch."

"Fair enough. Tomorrow?" He wanted to get that shower, the promise of sleeping together.

"Sounds good. Tonight we just crash."

"Mmm." And touch and lick…

"I can hear you, you know."

"Well, I hope so. That makes it nice, not to have to say it out loud." Kit winked broadly, making it a parody.

Mick pinched his ass, making him jump. "Don't make me beat you."

"You wouldn't. You might fuck me good and hard, but you wouldn't hurt me." He knew better. He felt the thread between them like a line.

Mick moaned. "I will, in fact, do that. Though with your fucking beautiful cock, I might throw you down and ride you this time. I love how thick and hot you get. I want to feel that."

He almost sagged to his floor. His alpha would trust him to do that…

Kit would tell Mick he'd never done that, but Mick knew.

I know, and it turns me on, Kit. That you're mine, that all these firsts are mine too.

Mick… His brain was mush, his legs wouldn't work, and his cock felt like a rock. A hot one.

"Mmm. Pretty bear." Mick stroked his hair, keeping him from ending up on the floor.

"Yours." Pretty. No one had ever said that to him before.

"You are. I want everything, Kit. I'm all in now that I've let myself have you." Mick looked at him, those dark eyes flashing gold, and his heart raced.

"All in. I love you, mate. I always have." He'd waited and waited, and it had been worth it. Every single second of it.

"Good." Mick kissed him then, stealing his breath, and he clung to Mick's wide shoulders, his need rising.

Your place. Please.

Our place, Kit.

Ours. He was going to cream his jeans.

Mick kept a tight hold on him, all but dragging him to their—their—apartment, and they barely made it inside before clothes started flying.

He wasn't sure if he wanted to laugh or moan or just jack off hysterically. Maybe all three.

At once.

"Nope. That's mine. No jacking off unless it's for me to watch."

Kit was learning all about how visual his mate was, how much he liked to watch. "I'd do it for you, but now I need touching."

"Bed," Mick barked, and they ran hand in hand, leaping into the bed. It groaned under their weight but held, and Mick was on top of him, grinding them together.

Kit took it—welcomed it, even—and he held them tight together.

Mick bit down on his neck, cock prodding his hip. "Kit. Baby."

"Yes." Whatever Mick needed, the answer was yes. The sound of his name when Mick said it like that made him wiggle and pant.

"What do you want this time, baby?"

"Anything. Absolutely anything. I just want to be with you."

"Good answer." Mick laughed, but the sound was sexy as hell, definitely naughty. Mick touched him, starting with his chest, sliding hands over his skin, rubbing thumbs across his nipples. They perked up, going hard as they got Mick's attention.

"You make me a little stupid."

"It goes both ways, baby. You've made me nuts for a long time." Mick nibbled on his neck.

"That's good. I'm glad. I want you to need me too." Kit lifted his chin and swallowed hard.

"I do. So much." Mick did a slow roll against him, muscles rippling, and that made his mouth dry and his ass clench. Somehow they were needing again, ramping each other up like they hadn't ever made love before.

This was all still so new.

Kit didn't think it would ever get old for him. Hell, how long had Brock and Grizz been mates? And they never seemed to tire.

"Don't bring them to bed with us."

Kit chuckled. "Sorry. I wasn't really thinking of *them*."

"I'd hate to bite you."

Kit pulled Mick's head up, focusing them together. "I've never wanted anyone but you. And I want you to bite."

"Damn. When you say things like that..."

"You used to think I was too inexperienced to know." He was poking the wolf.

Mick growled. "I know better. We're mates."

"We are." Kit believed it. He knew it, to the core.

"Hot as fire for me, baby." Mick didn't try to get inside him. They just lined up their cocks and started rubbing. Hard.

"Yes. Burning up." And Kit was grateful as fuck for it.

"Harder, yeah? More." Mick stroked against him, balls banging into him, and those teeth scored his neck again, which made him arch and rub and pant.

He reached down and squeezed their cock tips, driving them both that little bit higher.

Mick growled for him, and he could feel the pressure at the edge of his brain, could tell how close Mick was to coming. He grabbed that tight ass and yanked them together, wanting Mick's seed all over him, wanting to smell like his mate.

"Bear! Fuck. Gonna."

"Now, mate! Now!" He squeezed them both hard.

"Uhn!" Mick danced against him, coming hard, his scent flooding Kit's senses.

Every time got better, no matter what they did together.

And this was just the first few days.

The thought of how much more they had to explore sent him over the edge, just crashing past what he could hold in. He shot all over Mick's belly and thighs, mingling them together, and Mick moaned for him, pressing kisses all over his face.

"That's it, baby. That's perfect. So damn amazing."

He thought the fact that he got to stay here was the amazing part—that he got to sleep with Mick.

"We can clean up later," Mick mumbled against his neck, and then his type-A alpha lover was dozing right off, snoring on the same spot.

Kit smiled at the ceiling. Well, maybe he should say he got to hold Mick while he slept.

SIX

Mick slept for a little while but woke up with his mind racing. He didn't want to disturb Kit, who lay on his belly, butt up and nose down, one arm tossed across Mick's stomach.

But he did want to think on the Maldinado problem.

The guy always seemed to have specific timing for what he did. There would be these long stretches of inactivity, and then flurries of attacks and tying up loose ends. Now, some folks would probably say that the guy was a nutjob who liked elaborate schemes and needed time to set them up. Mick didn't buy that. Sure, the guy was escalating, and his last communique from Greg had said Maldinado was off his nut a mile, but—

So maybe he needed James to get lists of pertinent dates together and they would have Brock look and see if they meant anything to him.

They hadn't come at it from that angle yet.

He texted James, knowing that the tech guru would only be in bed if Hank insisted, and sure enough, James answered him.

<I need dates on the major events. Start with Rey's client dying, do Brock's thing with the warehouse, the croc attack. All of it.>

<No prob. Y?>

<hunch>

<love those. Gimme a few>

<You got it>

He could so snuggle.

"You're thinking hard."

"Did the smell of smoke wake you?" he teased.

"Yeah, it so did. What's up?" Kit yawned hugely, the move utterly bearlike.

"I want to see if there's any significance to the dates that Maldinado ramps up."

"You mean like he kills people on Brock's birthday?"

"Maybe? Maybe everything has a signifier. Maybe not. Maybe he's got a seasonal thing going. I just want to see if there's a pattern."

Every piece of information they could gather could be a weapon.

"That would be something—I mean if this is religious or something." Kit frowned, the wheels starting to turn.

"Yeah. Yeah, James is compiling a list. If Brock sees something, cool. If not, then I'll have you work with Rey to see what other pattern it might follow. You two are scary good at that."

He felt Kit's chest swell with a deep breath. He thought it was pride. "All those scary movies and video games."

"Is that what it is? Not just natural skill?" Mick was loving this playful side of Kit.

"Maybe a little. I've always been curious."

"I know." He had despaired sometimes when Kit was younger. He'd been into every damn thing. Now it was more than a little amazing.

Kit grinned, and there was more than a little evil in it. "It's a thing. That was a good early morning thought on your part though. People would think you're a PI."

Mick snorted. "Instead of a red-tape pusher? Yeah, those were the days."

Kit's head tilted. "Do you hate it? Managing?"

"No." No, Mick loved his team. "I just used to be able to do more investigative work before this shit with Maldinado. I kinda miss the balance."

"Yeah. I can help. I'm good at it—at paperwork and organization."

"You are." He grinned. "I wouldn't ask you to do the admin Carrie did, but maybe you can keep me on track with some of this shit the cops and Feds need."

"I can do whatever you need." Kit rubbed a line down his belly.

"I want to work with you, not against you." The threat of Kit leaving had made him hit the wall. He was in this for the long haul.

"I needed to be important to you."

"You always have been. I get something in my mind and it's hard to change." When Kit just chuckled, he shook his head. "Yeah, yeah, you all know me too well."

"It's my honor to." Kit squeezed his hand. No one ever had loved him like Kit.

Now he was going to return the favor.

"So. Cuddle. Wash up. Organize the office. Ride herd on the kitty and the fox."

"Yes. Then french toast and bacon. I need food." Kit waggled his eyebrows.

"French toast..." He did love maple syrup. "You're on, baby." Thank god they had amazing metabolisms.

Kit nodded and patted his belly. "I'm a growing mate."

"You so are. A berserker bear burns some calories."

That got him more laughter, which Mick was just enough of a sap to want. All of it all the time.

"That's me, man. The crazy ursine." Kit rolled up and rumbled happily.

"Mmm. Where are you going?"

"Potty. I'll wash my hands." Kit waggled his eyebrows and headed to the bathroom. Silly man.

Mick checked his phone again before resolutely putting it aside. Kit deserved his time, and they had to check with Brock once the dates were all run. And Grizz had rules about how much downtime he and Brock needed.

Mick got that now more than he ever had. There had to be work/life balance. He'd always been a little sad as his team started pairing up. Not jealous, but wistful, maybe…

Now, though, now he honestly knew the best was last.

Kit was magical.

Kit's pleasure flowed into their bond, which was growing every day. He must have heard that last thought. That was a fine thing. Mick meant every word.

All he wanted in the world right now was this Maldinado thing stopped, so he could bond with Kit, spend a few months resting and breathing and together.

"That sounds so yummy. Would you really do that?" Kit slid into bed with him again.

"I would. Rey can interview clients and collect payments and Dylan can assign cases and check on progress. You'd have to get Locke up to snuff on the garage, but we could do it." Without this constant threat, he would vacation like a fiend.

"I'm in. I have savings. I would help." Kit drew him in and wrapped around him.

"Then we could totally do it up right. Where have you always wanted to go?"

"Promise not to laugh?"

"Promise."

"Banff. In Canada, you know? It's like, an amazing place for bears."

God, that was adorable. "Really? I'm in. I've never looked at it."

"I know you like the mountains, so I think you would love it." Kit hopped up to bring back a laptop. He got a little show, the resort town, the national park.

"That looks amazing, baby. We could rent an Airbnb."

"Right? Somewhere safe to run and hunt, to roll around in our true forms?" Kit's eyes were lit up, dancing.

"Yes. And we can eat good food and be tourists and point at things." Hell, he just wanted to be able to sleep in. Until noon.

Kit nodded. "Sleep and sleep for hours. I'm so in."

"Then that's what we'll do. We'll get this guy, neutralize him, and go on vacay."

Kit pulled back to look at him. "Did you just say vacay?"

"You and Rey have had a terrible influence on me."

"Well, I've sure tried..." Kit chuckled, shaking his head.

"Then don't bitch, baby." He tickled Kit, who kicked and laughed and damn near knocked him off the bed.

"Bitch? Me?" Kit cackled, the sound wild and happy. "So mean to me."

"I am. I'm a dictator. A big, grumpy wolf." Mick rolled them away from the edge of the mattress.

"Grump, grump, grump..." Kit nibbled his ear.

"That's me." He grabbed that fine ass.

Mick amended his plan. Get busy with Kit. Then cuddles. Then breakfast.

SEVEN

K it flipped french toast. He loved how it made Mick smile when he made it, so he was all over it. Rey had volunteered to make bacon, saying James was crazy obsessed with making the timeline Mick had requested.

"James only does obsessed; you know that." Kit knew better, but it felt good to tease.

"I know! And that's good, right? But he does good work."

"He does amazing work. You know how I feel about him. I was joking."

"I know!" Rey poked him. "We're all a little on edge, huh? This whole situation is nuts. I like the idea of Maldinado having some sort of schedule though. Then we can figure it out and get ahead."

"Yeah. Yeah, Mick woke up thinking about it. His brain is something special."

"It is. He's a good boss. And you two! Like, on fire." Rey was tickled for him. He could tell. That quicksilver grin lit up Rey's copper eyes. "Finally."

"Right? All I had to do was threaten to leave..."

Rey chuckled. "Wolves are hardheaded."

"You should know." He flipped the bread. Rey had mated with wolf PI Dylan and never looked back. Dylan was an ex-cop, and he could be seriously heel diggy.

"I do! I know all about it." Rey winked at him, red eyebrows waggling furiously.

He laughed. Foxes could be pretty stubborn too. Rey could put his relatively small foot down hard. "Thanks for helping me cook. Mick is coming, but he got a call from that Fed again. The undercover guy is a friend, so he's really worried." Mick had told him he could stay, but he wasn't one to eavesdrop. Mick would fill them in.

"It's always something, isn't it? Has it always been that way?" Rey asked over his shoulder.

Kit thought about that, trying to remember anything that had happened before Maldinado came into their lives. Some-times it seemed like they all began there. "Sort of, but not really. Not so much."

"Yeah, that's what Dylan seems to think too. He's been here longest besides you. I mean, me, I brought it with me." Rey gave him an agonized look. Rey had come to them to help figure out who had killed a client, having no idea it was the tip of the iceberg.

"No, fox. Someone brought it to you. Mmm. Bacon." Brock nuzzled Rey's hair on the way by.

"Someone just made sure you were going to show up here." Kit thought that was the more logical situation. "You were led here."

Rey gave Brock a sad look. "I feel awful that I was instru-mental, no matter what."

"Bah." Grizz followed Brock in, the big grizzly's nose working. "You've been an asset. If Maldinado knew how much help you were, he would take you out. So we'll keep it our secret, but you're a star."

"Right. That's me. Foxy star of sparkly wonder."

"You read my mind, babe." Dylan came in, eyes bright. "You forgot one part though."

"Did I?"

"Yes, love. Mine."

Oh, how sweet.

He didn't feel even the slightest pang. In fact, he could hear Mick, who was fretting, but off the phone and on his way. He wanted that maple syrup.

"Is Hank staying with James? Do I need to take them plates?" Kit asked.

"I will." Rey put the last bacon on paper towels to drain. "I'm quick as a bunny."

"My quick brown fox." Dylan goosed Rey on the way by.

"That's it. Good thing you're not a lazy dog." Rey took two plates, these with salted caramel instead of maple. The cats did like their salt.

He dished up, loving that somehow they were all coming together again. Like the tide was turning. It gave him hope that they were onto something with the dates.

He wasn't sure what was going to happen to all of them if it was a lie. He just wasn't sure they could handle it.

So they would put all they had into this.

Brock sat, looking a little battered, but his mind was working hard. Kit could tell.

Mick strode in, shaking his head. "Greg has gone silent. No one has heard from him on his last two scheduled check-ins."

"Oh, no!" He handed off serving to Dylan and went to hug Mick. "What do we do?"

"We let him do his job." Brock's voice was hard, dull, miserable.

"We do. He knows the risks. Then again, he might be in deep enough that he's worried about checking in and tipping them off. So we let it ride."

Mick kissed Kit, then went to hug Brock hard. "You know this too. You've done the work."

"I have." Brock sighed. "Are you telling me to stop the drama?"

"Yeah." Mick slapped his back. "Now, where's my food."

"*Were's* the wolf's food?" Dylan teased.

"Shifting in the pan!" Grizz added.

"Gimme." Mick stalked to the stove, and they all laughed.

Kit pushed him aside, then made Mick up a plate. He made his, too, checking to ensure everyone was fed before he sat with Mick. Rey was there and on Dylan's lap in no time, so they were all munching away.

He felt like this was the first time. The moment he fit in, too, all the way. Kit was going to try to enjoy every second.

Mick grinned at him. "Just enough cinnamon, baby."

"Thanks. Rey did a good job on the bacon too."

"He always does."

"So what do we do while we wait for James?" Dylan asked. "My case wrapped."

"Mine did too," Locke said.

"I have a few new ones to hand out," Mick said, "but first you're all going to help Kit move in with me."

"Dude." Locke stood there for a second, and then his happy laughter filled the room. "You finally did it!"

"Yeah, yeah." Mick's cheeks went red, but he didn't deny it, did he? "So I move slow. I'm old."

"You're the boss. You had to make sure he was studly enough for you."

"Shit. I had to tell myself it wasn't wrong to want him." Mick looked at him, and Kit melted at the deep need he saw in Mick's eyes.

"Aww... Oh, yay. Kit! Yay!" Rey grabbed him and hugged him tight.

Kit chuckled, but he was about to bust with pride and

happiness. Not only was he moving in, but Mick was telling the world.

This was—this was the best dream, the real dream.

"So? Let's do this." Brock bounced up, clapping his hands. "Any opportunity to snoop is a good one."

"Stay out of my underwear, kitty," he warned.

"What?" Brock made wide eyes. "Dios, you get into someone's stuff once… Not my fault you were hiding catnip."

"For James's birthday!"

"I shared!" Brock grabbed him and hugged him. "Me? I'm soon, too, eh? My birthday."

"I will provide catnip." But Kit looked at Mick over Brock's head.

Three days, mate. His birthday is in three days.

Rock on. Good to know. Brock was harder to know, harder to understand, but he was family.

Mick kind of rolled his eyes, but Kit had no idea what he meant, and now was not the time to talk about it. Brock looked happy for the first time in ages.

"What are you going to do with the space, Mick?" Dylan asked, almost loping down the hall.

"Well, we talked about a gaming room," Mick said. "Movie-room type thing. That way the lounge can be for eating and stuff."

"Yeah? Like a media thing? I'll spring for the chairs. Rey would love that."

"Good deal. Then that's what we'll do. When you and I just want to play cards…"

Dylan laughed. "Right? We get the kitchen table and they can go be loud."

Kit snorted. "Everyone came to my place to be loud, you grumpy wolves. So it will get much the same use."

"Yeah, but it'll smell less like bear farts!" Dylan howled with laughter.

"Ew!"

Before long, they were all tramping back and forth, taking Kit's stuff to Mick's apartment. Theirs now. Kit was floating.

I like it.

He looked over at Mick. *What?*

I like that smile on your face.

Thank you. It means a lot, that you told everyone.

You mean a lot to me. I want them all to know. Mick's eyes flashed gold.

They all do. He squeezed Mick's fingers, then went to pack his books up.

Rey got his video games, Dylan his console. His clothes only took two trips. It was all moved in no time, him and Locke hauling the biggest stuff. Bear power.

Soon it was done, and he was standing in Mick's apartment, utterly shocked.

The others left them, and he looked at his stuff fitting in with Mick's and tried to catch his breath.

"Not having second thoughts, are you?" Mick asked, coming to slide both arms around him.

"No. It's hard to believe it's real." He leaned back because it was easy to believe Mick was real.

"Yeah, well, if I start to get too overbearing again, hit me. I want you to be happy."

"I'm yours. That's what I need." Simple as that.

"Don't sell yourself short." Mick stroked his belly. "You get to make some demands."

"Do I? Like snuggles and morning orgasms?"

"Yeah. See, now that's the kind of thing I aspire to give." Mick nibbled his shoulder.

That was a perfect sting. Absolutely, and he tilted his head to get more.

"Mmm. Kit." Mick bit, then licked to ease it, then licked again. The mix of sensations were making him crazed.

He didn't want Mick to stop, so he made sure his wolf had access. He tilted his head forward, which pushed his ass back.

Mick rubbed against him, moaning, and he felt every bit of that hardness pressing to him. That was something else, how much Mick wanted him.

"Where are we going to start, Mick? Over the sofa? Over the table?"

"Over the table. It's closer and clean." His clothes were partly on the sofa. "I found your secret stash of lube…"

"Did you?" Oh goddess. That meant he'd found—

"And your dildo. You like wolf cock, do you?"

He was going to burn to a cinder. "I do. I fantasized. What can I say? The real thing is so, so much better." Might as well be honest. He didn't believe in hiding things from Mick.

"Good. I want you to want it, baby." Mick rubbed a hand over his dick, then moved him toward the table to bend him over it. "I want you to feel me, everywhere."

He was in. All the way. Whatever Mick gave him, he'd taken.

Mick yanked Kit's pants down, then kicked his legs apart. It sounded all rough trade, but Mick was remarkably gentle about it. Then those hard fingers pried his ass cheeks apart.

"You look sweet and pink, ready to be slicked."

When Mick swooped down and licked his hole, he roared, utterly shocked.

That had—only in porn. He'd never even dared to fanta-size about this. Mick was a natural too. Goddess.

Breathe. I have you. I want you to feel everything.

He nodded. Everything. He wanted to feel everything too.

He bent farther, pushing back and out with his hips, begging for more. Mick gave it to him, really pushing in to test him, taste him. He'd never felt so sensual, so intensely sexual.

Kit swore his knees were going to melt.

Mick licked and licked, fondling his balls until he wanted to scream.

He panted, trying not to explode. "Mick. Please. I need it."

Need what, baby?

"You. Your cock. Please. Let's come together." He stretched out long across the table, his toes curling with the sheer pleasure.

"So fucking hot." Mick slid up along his legs and thighs, mouth on his back. Wet fingers slid into him, two at once, opening him right up, making his muscles sing with pleasure-pain.

"Love!" He bit out the word, canting his hips to take Mick even deeper.

"On fire inside." Mick's growl buzzed along his spine, making him rock back and forth.

"Not enough. I need your dick."

"Not going to hurt you. Not for anything in the world."

He moaned, the rush of heat and love from Mick's words huge, echoing inside him. They felt huge, but not as big as Mick's cock, which stretched him until he shouted when Mick pulled those fingers free and glided into him.

That dildo had nothing on his mate.

Nothing.

He pushed himself up and back, driving back onto Mick's fat needy cock. It felt huge inside him and hot as a brand. Mick was made for him, fitting him perfectly, and Kit knew he'd never get enough.

"Damn, baby. Damn. I want more of you every time I have you. You make me crazy. I could just eat you up."

"What big teeth you have, Mr. Wolf."

"The better to nibble you with, my love," Mick growled in his best Grimm's voice. It should have been hilarious and deflating, but it was hot and adorable instead. Mick was playing with him, and it made him seem younger and happier.

"Love you." It seemed like the only, the right thing to say. He braced himself, his sweat-slick hands slipping on the table.

"I love you, too, baby." Mick's teeth sank into his shoulder, and he shouted, his balls pulling up.

Mick fucked him hard, in and out, in and out. He felt every tiny movement, every inch of Mick inside him. It was perfect. Not enough and too much at the same time. Maddening. His entire universe tightened to his hole, to the wild rub of Mick inside him.

All he could do was hang on and beg, words spilling out of him, babbling. Mick was relentless, like a flame against his skin, those sharp teeth never letting up on his neck and shoulders.

He clenched tight, squeezing Mick as hard as he could, demanding that his alpha fill him.

Mick slammed deep inside him, and he shouted again when the tip of Mick's cock hit his sweet spot. He came so hard and so fast it left him breathless, his body jerking and dancing.

Then Mick was barking out his own pleasure, coming deep inside, and Kit felt every little pulse of wet heat.

"Fuck, baby. Fuck, that's good. Ungh."

All he could do was nod and pant. Nothing else.

He was proud that he hadn't fallen to the floor.

"Come to bed with me, love. Our bed." They had moved Mick's smaller, older bed out and put on clean sheets when they moved Kit's in.

"Ours. Thank you, for letting me in, for saying yes." He loved that he'd provided the place where they would sleep.

"I wouldn't want a separate living space from my mate." Mick slid free slowly, and they cleaned up a little before padding to the bedroom. "Sleep with me a bit, love. I have a feeling things are about to get busy. An itch on the back of my neck."

Shit. Mick's itches were legendary.

"Then we'd better enjoy things now, while we can."

"We'd better. I can think of a dozen more ways in between wolf and bear naps."

"No, no. Bear naps are bad. They go on and on."

Mick hooted. "Then we'll think like the cats, baby, and sleep with one eye open."

Kit was smiling as he sank down on the bed. "That sounds perfect."

EIGHT

Mick woke up in the middle of the night, his heart pounding. Something they'd said right before they moved Kit in with him was ringing in his ears.

Brock's birthday was in three days.

Well. Two now. Or was it still three?

He grabbed his phone. <You got that timeline?>

<Yep> James came back. <Bring coffee>

Right. At this time of the morning, they would need it.

He poked Kit in the ribs. "James has run the timeline."

"Okay. I'll make coffee. We going up or are they coming down?" Kit was up and moving, and Mick was ninety-nine percent sure that his bear wasn't awake yet.

"We'll go up so he has all his screens and shit." He scratched his belly as he sat up. Was he too gross? Nah. As early as it was, James would be less than fresh too. Mick would bet James's mate Hank was snoring in a corner of the office.

Kit blundered around, grunting and dancing a little as he tried to put trousers on.

The dancing bear. That was pretty amazing, and Mick stopped to watch fondly.

He had to admit, Kit could do more asleep than anyone he'd ever met.

They headed to James's office together after making coffee, Kit yawning. "I hope he wants coffee."

"This is caffeine kitty you're talking about."

"Yeah, I know. Meow."

They staggered into James's inner sanctum, both of them yelping at the bright lights when they hit their eyes. "Jesus, James. Do you ever sleep?"

"He's about to," Hank growled. "He may not know it, but he is."

James blinked at them owlishly. "But first, bar graphs and mind maps."

"Show me. Tell me there's a pattern."

"Fuck. There's a pattern. Look."

The graphs were shockingly regular. They were flat, then a huge spike, then a lull, a smaller spike, another lull, a mid-sized spike, then another huge one. That pattern repeated, three times.

"Okay. Okay." Kit came over to hand him a cup of coffee. "Look. This is Brock's birthday. This is what you were trying to tell me last night, right, Mick?"

"It was my thought, yeah, but Brock was in such a good mood..." Mick stared. "What are the other dates, I wonder."

"We need to ask Brock." Hank was in a mood. "It's time for him to just tell us, dammit."

"It is. Do we pull an intervention?" Kit asked.

"No. No, I think faced with this, he'll give us the whole story." To be fair to Brock, he hadn't known about the jaguar shifter thing, he didn't think. What Maldinado had been trying to make him into.

"What story?"

Dylan and Brock came in, followed by Rey and Grizz.

He blinked, and Dylan shrugged. "The energy around here is intense."

"Yeah." Grizz put a hand on Brock's shoulder, guiding him to a chair. "Spill."

James motioned to the chart on the big screen, and Brock studied it, the color draining from his face. "Dios. I knew it was about me, but this is insane."

"I know the spikes are your birthday, but—"

Locke snarled. "He stole Brock from me on his birthday."

They all looked at the big bear, then at Brock, who sighed. "I haven't been holding back because I don't trust you, amigos. It's because it was humiliating and awful, and it gives me nightmares."

Kit went to hug him, and Grizz let him in. "I'm so sorry, Brock. But we have to hear it all."

Brock chewed his lower lip, seeming to shrink, looking like anything but his slinky, confident black-ops self.

"I think he slipped me something, but I had no clue at the time. Locke and I snarled about something—I don't even remember what now—and then there was someone willing to listen." Brock sighed and shook his head. "I was in his bed in the morning. And I stayed there. I never tried to get out. Every time I thought about leaving, he was there telling me to stay."

"I thought you just—fell for him." Locke's wide shoulders went up around his ears. "That you really thought he was your mate."

"He had me convinced for a long while. I—" Brock took a deep breath. "Now that I know what a whiz he is at developing drugs, it makes more sense."

"How did you get away? I mean, he wanted to make you some weird super soldier." Mick could chew nails he was so pissed on Brock's behalf.

"On our first anniversary, the torture started. I couldn't shift. He kept me caged under the bed; he shot me up with the nobenime. It made me want to do as I was told, but it had side effects. It made me frustrated, and I'd have convulsions." Brock's voice didn't shake, but the shame there rocked Mick to the core. "I overheard him one day, saying he was giving me the maximum dose on my birthday, and I had to get out before that happened."

"I'm glad you did." Kit petted and fretted.

Grizz growled. "If I ever get a chance to get my hands on him."

"We'll tear him apart, Locke. Prison isn't gonna work for this guy. He needs to be neutralized." Mick wasn't gonna apologize for being bloodthirsty.

"He kept me in a cage, humiliated me, used me as a sex toy," Brock whispered. "But he got careless the night before he was going to give me the big dose—excited, I suppose—and the lock didn't latch all the way. I never looked back."

"No. No looking back." Mick didn't think Brock would survive that.

"No." Grizz gently moved Kit out of the way and gathered Brock into his arms. "None. We look at the patterns and get a step ahead."

Rey cleared his throat. "Right. So you can see a small flurry of activity on the days leading up to your birthday, Brock, but then the croc attack happened on the day. The building fell. So he was trying to get to you or something to do with you."

Brock frowned, and then his head tilted. "This is his birthday, and this is the day his unit threw him out."

Those dates corresponded with Patel getting sprung from prison and an attack on the building.

Brock stood, going to trace lines on the screen. "I need a printout of this."

"Of course. Totally. Whatever you want." James nodded, the mountain lion beginning to fade.

"Go sleep. Rey can print this out, right?" Mick said.

"Of course." Rey sat in his work chair and rolled over like a billiard ball, knocking James away from his workstation. "Buh bye. Hank?"

"On it." Hank took James into his arms. "Bed."

"I—" James frowned, and Hank growled.

"Say good night, Gracie."

"Good night, Gracie."

They all chuckled, even Brock. He was pale but composed. Mick had never realized how fragile Brock was. He had always seemed like the cool and composed hired gun, but Joao Maldinado had done a number on his friend.

Now that he knew what was coming, and when? He was going to do a number on a certain psychopathic fox.

"Let's get a list of possible dates and events, guys." Rey handed out printed sheets and highlighters. "We need to be on the ready."

"We know when it's coming. Just a couple of days." Brock sighed heavily. "My fucking birthday."

"Yeah. We just need to figure out what he'll think is an appropriate action. I wish your undercover guy wasn't in the wind," Dylan said.

Mick agreed. If Greg could even give them a hint of what was moving in Maldinado's organization, it would be a huge help. But he was out of touch. "We'll have to move ahead like he won't help. There's no way around that."

"Okay." Kit grabbed his sheets. "Let's do this." He looked up. "We're going to need food."

"I'll handle that," Dylan said. "You all read."

And just like that, they were all acting like PIs again.

Even if they were working on their own case.

NINE

K it needed to go to the auto parts store.

He didn't want to bring it up to Mick. He'd finally gotten his lover to go to sleep for a bit, and that was great, but Kit was restless, so he'd gone to work in the garage.

Their big van needed a bunch of work. But only if he could go get the parts.

He ran into Rey out in the hall on the way up to the main lounge, where he'd hoped to find someone to go with him. Mick had said no one went out without a buddy, and he was trying to follow that rule. They had two days until Brock's birthday, so he should be okay.

"Hey, I need to go to the auto parts store. Do you think Dylan would go with me?"

Rey rolled his eyes. "Mick assigned him that new client. He's on a Zoom."

"Faboo. Dammit. You want to come with me?"

"God, do I ever. This place smells like farts, and everyone is in a crap mood."

A laugh burst out of him. "You said it. I just need to get outside for an hour."

"We need groceries. Let's go for two hours."

"I'll leave Mick a text once we're on our way, fair enough?" Rey wasn't useless, but he wasn't sure his mate would approve.

"Yes. That's the same thing I will do with Dylan." Rey looked so tickled, unholy glee glowing in his copper eyes. He did love some mischief. And he did have that foxy scream if things went tits up.

"Cool. Come on." He grabbed his jacket and headed down toward the garage, going for stealthy.

"Where are you two going?" Brock popped out of the admin office downstairs, almost making him pee himself.

Rey staggered, hand to his heart. "You nearly gave me a heart attack!"

"Why are you lurking in the office?" he demanded, trying to look less guilty.

"I was looking through Carrie's records. She's very analog as well as digital. I thought maybe we had repair records on the old building that might shed some light on the way they knew how to make it collapse."

Oh, sure, make them feel guilty for playing hooky by working.

"Cool. Did you find anything?" Rey asked, and Kit fought the urge to get them moving again.

"I'm not sure. There are a couple of maintenance receipts not from accounts we normally used. I need to call her. Where are you going, amigos?"

Brock was focused for a kitty.

He and Rey exchanged looks. "We need parts for the van," he finally said.

"And groceries," Rey added.

"Nao. The two of you are not going alone."

The flat refusal made him grit his teeth. He wanted to say, "Okay, Mick," but he didn't. Brock was right to be worried. They all had crosshairs on them. That didn't mean that things needed to fall apart.

"I won't let anything happen to Rey, Brock. I swear. We're going to get parts, food, and we'll be back." Kit wasn't a child, and he wasn't reckless.

"Mmm. Nao. I will come with you."

He tilted his head. "Is that wise? Maybe you should stay in until after your birthday." Brock was the biggest walking target of all of them. It seemed crazy for him to just leave the building when they had proven it was a tough nut to crack.

"If you want to go, I go with you. Or I will go tell Mick."

"Mick's asleep." He would rather not go than wake his mate up. "Like genuinely asleep."

"So is Locke."

That was good. Grizz had been full of rage after the revelations about what Maldinado had done to Brock.

They had a stare down for a long minute. Then Rey threw up his hands. "Let's all go so we can get back before someone stops us!"

Kit chuckled. "Agreed."

Brock patted his pocket. "I already have my wallet. Come on." The jaguar rolled his eyes. "I'm dying for some chicken nuggets. Who's driving?"

"I will." Kit loved to drive.

"Good." Brock grinned. "I'll take shotgun."

"Aw, man." Rey stuck out his tongue. "You suck. I knew I should have called it."

"You need your booster seat, foxy." Brock ruffled Rey's hair as they headed down. They took the big armored SUV since they didn't have to blend in on surveillance.

"Yeah, yeah, yeah. I'm little, but I'm mighty." Rey stuck his tongue out and wiggled his eyebrows.

"You are. Your scream can stop the world." Brock said it with pure admiration.

"I try. Let's go to find Kit his toys." Rey blew Kit a kiss.

"And food." Kit grinned, excited to be playing hooky.

They headed out, making sure the garage closed behind them. No sense in taking stupid risks.

They laughed and chatted together, all of them seeming casual, but Kit knew they were on high alert just like he was. They weren't acting as bait on purpose, but there was always a chance.

There was a part of him that was worried that they'd come for Mick when he was gone. Just an itch, but they couldn't just hide, right?

James and Hank were there. They were like a well-oiled machine. Really. Locke was strong too. Their grizzly. They would be fine.

Kit took a circuitous route to the store, relaxing enough to turn the radio on.

Rey sang, and even Brock hummed, and the auto parts place took like, ten minutes once Kit convinced the bored sales guy he knew what he needed. They always wanted to look things up for him by make and model.

He had this. Seriously. The guy turned to get the parts, and there was something...something weird.

Something off.

"Brock?" he whispered, and to his utter relief, the big cat nodded, herding them toward the door.

"Now."

Kit grabbed Rey and yanked him toward the door, his sixth sense in full itch.

The shots blew out the windows of the auto parts store, and Kit shoved Rey to the ground, trying to get low. They had to get to the Hummer. They had to. It was armored, and they could take off, hell-bent for leather.

They all scrambled, and just as they cleared the front door, the Hummer went up in what looked like a mushroom cloud, the shockwave knocking him back into a plate-glass window.

"Run! Run now!"

He heard Brock's voice like his head was wrapped in cotton, and he blinked up, swaying, trying to focus, to understand.

Rey was crumpled, unconscious, and he couldn't just leave him. Kit grabbed him, shielding him.

Then the second explosion happened, something slammed into his head, and the whole world went black.

———

A wild banging dragged Mick up from a dead sleep.

"Boss! Boss! I need you! Goddamn it, Mick! WAKE YOUR ASS UP!"

"What?" His head hurt. God, his head hurt.

Mick tried to sit up, and he gagged, grabbing his skull with both hands.

"What!"

"Please!" That was James and he was screaming. *Fuck. Fuck. Get up. Get your wolfy ass up.*

Mick dragged his butt out of bed and all but crawled to the door. "What the fuck, James?" he croaked when he threw open the door. "I'm dying here."

"The Hummer exploded. I got the alarm. The Hummer exploded at an auto parts store. The cops are there!" James's legs gave out under him.

"What?" Why couldn't he say anything else? "The Hummer was at the auto parts..."

Mick stopped, swaying. Kit. Auto parts.

"Kit. Brock. Rey. They all went together. The police didn't find any bodies. I need help. Please."

Mick roared, racing past James to the garage downstairs. It was as if he had to see for himself that the Hummer was gone. He choked again, his body feeling like someone had beaten him with a tire iron.

"Kit!" He shouted it mentally as well as physically, desperately searching for his mate.

From the stairwell, he heard a wild howl from Dylan, and then he was bowled over by Grizz, who slammed into the bay doors in pure bear form.

"Shit!" He hit hard and skidded on his ass. "Grizz! Grizz, no!" Their Locke was trying to rip the doors down. "We can't leave James and Hank unprotected! The doors have to stay up."

Locke roared, the sound absolute agony.

"Alpha!" Dylan came to him. "They have them. We have to go. We have to find him. He's *not dead*!"

"Stop. Dylan, stop." He dragged his ass up again. "We will. We'll get them back." He wanted to lose his shit, but he couldn't. Locke and Dylan and even James were doing that for him. Kit wasn't dead. He couldn't be. There were no bodies. "He has them, so we have to get them. James. We need any and all video. I'll call the cops. Locke." He barked at the big bear. "Conserve your energy. You'll need it."

Locke's eyes rolled, but the human wouldn't come. Not even a bit.

Fuck him. "Upstairs. I need intel. Where the fuck is Hank?"

"Here, boss. On the horn with one of my CIs. We're looking for a panel van, blue, heading west on I-70."

"Good man. I need to get outfitted. Dylan, get us a vehicle ready to go. One he can fit in if need be." Mick jerked a thumb at Locke. "Hank, you stay here with James. We can't take a chance on you two getting drugged. We need to be on the road ASAP."

"I'll keep comms running with him. I swear. I'm not Rey, but I can talk with folks and get intel."

"I know. I know, man. You're good. My head."

"That means Kit got knocked out, Alpha." That was Dylan. He would know. Rey had been kidnapped before. "That's actually a good sign."

Mick would cling to that. Hard.

Locke vocalized, the sound utterly agonized, and Mick understood. This whole thing was about torture, about Brock, and now—

They'd all failed.

The motherfucker had Brock.

They had to get him back before Maldinado started the drugging process. They had to. There was no way their Brazilian wild child was going to become some jaguar god's avatar and be a zombie shape-shifter.

No fucking way.

Ten

K it's brain spun, the fog there refusing to part, to let the clear air in. He wasn't sure where he was, but he knew he was hurting, he knew he was moving, and he knew something was wrong.

He tried to pry his eyes open, but as soon as the light started to creep in, he felt a stabbing pain in his head. Concussion? He let the medic inside him take over. Yeah, Possible concussion. Bruised everywhere. His wrist was broken.

He sucked in a slow, careful breath, trying to sniff out whatever information he could manage. He smelled ozone and ash, coppery blood, and gasoline, but underneath that, there was Rey and Brock. His pack.

Where was he? They were moving. Some kind of transport then. He rubbed his cheek against what he lay on. Carpet. A van? Was he chained? Kit twisted his wrists. Metal of some sort. No zip ties for the bear. That was smart but disappointing. Plastic he might have snapped, even with his wrist all a mess.

Of course, if he beared out, he wasn't sure even cuffs would hold him.

That was a good thought. He finally cracked one eye open, not enough to look like he was awake, he hoped. He saw Rey on his side opposite him, a huge bruise marring one cheek, blood on his lips. He was solidly out, his body fully limp.

Dammit. He needed to be able to shift, and he needed to be able to move and get them all going.

He worked his nose again, hunting scents outside the van. The driver stank of fear sweat. He didn't want to be on this job. There was no sign of Maldinado, he thought. That fox would smell like musk and jungle.

"Rey," he whispered. He needed his friend to wake up and prove he was in there.

He waited, and Rey never moved. But he did hear a soft grunt, and he dared to move his head slightly to see.

Brock. Unlike him and Rey, Brock was trussed like a mummy, arms and legs, a gag in his mouth. Someone had orders. Brock, as far as Maldinado was concerned, was both the dangerous one and the prize.

"Brock. Can you hear me? Are you in there?"

Brock's eyes popped open, bloodshot and furious but there.

Okay. Okay. Brock was alive. Yay.

"We have to get out of here." He had to figure this shit out.

Brock could barely move his head the way he was tied, but he inclined it as best he could. Okay, so Brock was with him. Good.

Rey blinked then, and he licked his lips, so he was on his way. "Quiet, Rey. Don't let them know you're awake." They had to figure out where they were going and get word to the rest of the team. Then they had to get each other out of their bonds enough to fight.

They had faced worse than this.

He thought. He hoped. No, he knew. Crocs were worse than one sweaty dude in a van.

Kit struggled to sit up, trying to stay as quiet as he could, but his head began to scream as he lifted it, and he heard *Kit! Kitkitkitkitkitkitkitkit!*

His eyes went wide, and the fog closed back in again, leaving him in silence.

Eleven

"I heard him." Mick was almost ready to head back to the garage. "James, I heard him."

James was back in his office, having outfitted them quickly with comms. "Good. That's good. Last sighting was at 70 and the Central Avenue bridge."

"Find them on the cameras."

"Every cop and Fed in town is on it, boss," Hank said. He and Dylan had loaded Locke into their own big van, which was rated to carry a bear or two. He was lying as still as death, his chest barely rising and falling. But that was deceptive. Locke could explode into action in seconds, and he would have the rage to do it.

"Find them!" Dylan searched the screens. "Goddamn it, James. Please!"

"I'm trying, Dyl. I swear to god."

"We can head that way. Let's go." He led Dylan out. No sense in sitting and fretting. James knew his job, and he had Hank, who had an in with Cole and the Feds.

Mick wished to hell he knew where Greg was in the undercover scheme, but for all he knew, the guy was dead.

They climbed into the van with Locke, and Dylan gave him a look. "We can do this."

"We will. I didn't take Kit as my mate finally just to lose him."

"And Kit's not letting you go either. You know it."

Locke rolled up. Caught in a half-form, the sight was terrifying, and his voice was barely understandable.

"Move. He moves."

"I'm on it, Grizz, man. I won't let that bastard have him." He was the crazy one behind the wheel, so he went for it. Dylan had cop skills, but he was too law-abiding. Mick would take that on-ramp on two fucking wheels.

"Fox hurt. Kit out. Bound."

"What? My fox?" Dylan turned. "Brock is conscious? Dammit, man, shift!"

Locke's roar damn near knocked the van off the road.

Mick kept them between the lines, barely, and Locke finally lay panting on the van floor. Dylan threw a blanket over him.

"Where?" Mick barked.

"Stay on...70 West," Locke ground out. "Still on highway."

"Kit and Rey?"

"Kit's got a serious head injury. Rey's still out."

Dylan made an agonized noise. "He needs to be okay."

"They're going to torture them," Locke snarled. "There's no more okay. You know what bear paws go for?"

"Stop it," Mick snapped, because it was that or puke. "They're smart and strong. They can hold on and we're on them." He was going to kill something. Hopefully soon.

Dylan nodded. "We will. We're coming and Brock knows it. Brock's pure evil, Rey is fast, and Kit's a fucking bear. He killed a weregator. A *gator*."

Grizz nodded, chin firming. "You're right. Brock knows who he is now. I—I'm just trying not to lose it."

"Good man. No losing it." Mick got it. He was dying a little inside every minute his team was gone. And this was his *mate*.

"They're slowing down. We've got to be close. I can hear him."

"Good. Keep listening." He wanted Grizz mind-melded with Brock as much as possible. "James? Hank? Any eyes."

Hank gave him an exit number, and hope surged in him. Okay, they were fairly close, making much better time than their prey. Someone was in no real hurry, which told him Maldinado wasn't at the end location right now. If he was waiting, they would be in a rush.

"Boss, they're slowing down in an industrial section. Warehouses." James sounded worn through.

"Give me an address." He knew James had to be dealing with an adrenaline crash. Ever since he'd been drugged and hurt so badly, he related poorly to this kind of stress. But he had to hang in—

Mick heard the sound of the crash before he felt it. Then he felt it, and he thought his bones might rattle for the rest of his life.

"Fuck!" Dylan bounced off the side of the inside of the van, grunting.

Hold it together, boss. He heard Kit in his skull, just as loud and cheery as hell, so he knew it wasn't real.

He swerved, but the sound of the front right tire smashing into the concrete divider was like a death knell. He knew the van was toast.

"Locke! You go get them. You and Dylan shift and run. I'll slow them down as best I can." He spoke on as they spun, the van going like a top.

"Boss!"

"Go!" He would do what he could. Someone had to get to their guys before Maldinado. "James, I need swarms of cops."

"Swarms."

They came to rest, and he grabbed the pistol out of the glove box, trying desperately to give his pack a chance.

He needed to lay down some fire as Locke and Dylan burst out of the van, snarling, running like fiends.

"Go! Find them!"

He'd be damned if he let his pack lose anything else.

———

Kit woke up when the truck stopped, and he heard gunfire blasting in the distance, smelled the ozone of the flash.

Fuck. Fuck. What did he do? He needed to save them all. Now.

He could feel Mick in his aching head, shouting obscenities. That was— where was Mick? There was gunfire in there too.

Mick? Mick, don't get shot.

Kit?

Don't. Get. Shot.

He couldn't handle that.

I've got three stooges following me. Drawing them away from you so there's less to deal with. I need you to get the others out.

I will. I—I will. Him? Fuck. How the hell was he supposed to do that? Kit wasn't sure he could focus both eyes.

I know your head hurts, but you can do this. You have to, baby. I trust you.

I love you. He heard doors opening somewhere, and he forced himself to stay limp and relaxed.

"Come on, you assholes. Let's get a move on. The boss wants these guys separated."

He cracked an eye, shocked as hell to see Greg, Mick's cop buddy standing there. But was that Greg? Was it the shapeshifter? Was Greg under the influence of nobenime?

"Where do we put this one? I think he's a bear, man. That cage we have isn't rated for that." That was the glunky driver.

"Shit, he's out. You all but bashed in his skull. There's no way he can shift." Greg's voice held an edge that made Kit listen. "I'll take the cat. The boss wants him on the drugs right away, and you're likely to be affected."

So, the driver was some sort of cat.

"You want me to kill the fox?"

"Nope. Boss wants this one to see this little one suffer. Toss him in with the bear."

Oh thank god.

"Are you sure?"

"Yeah. Boss says the bear goes nuts if he does shift. But he'll never hurt the fox."

"Oh, good idea."

He fought the urge to laugh. Greg was perfect, giving them every chance to get set up in a good position. So he had to trust that the man had their backs.

Greg is here.

Good deal. He expected to feel this wave of relief from Mick, but he felt the confidence Mick had in him instead.

I don't know where the face shifter is. He was at the store.

Keep your sniffer ready. He ought to smell off. Sour. Sick.

Right. They'd all read up and the drug cocktail Maldinado was giving this guy should make him stink. Bad. They'd all smelled it with the tiger Patel.

They moved him and Rey, and he knew he had no time at all to pull this off, and when he heard, *Dylan and Locke are coming. If you can do something, do it; you're running out of time,* he knew he was right.

He waited, biding his time until all they left was one bored guy to watch them. They would wait until he and Rey were awake to torture them. So he took a deep breath and moved Rey to one long edge of the cage, making no noise.

If you can, foxy, please wake up. If you can't, I will get you out of here.

Rey's lips moved, his brows drawing together. Woo. Okay, that was good.

He closed his eyes, waiting until the man was as far away as possible before letting his bear come in a rush. The cage pressed against his body, the cuffs against his wrists, before they both shattered.

The cage started to fall apart, and he caught the panel that wasn't leaning against the wall, his claws scraping the bars.

He had a shifted fox nosing him out of the cage before he could blink.

Good job.

He tried to put the cage down easy, but there was no way. None.

So he sent it flying, taking the running guard out with a thud and a clatter. The other guys were still hopefully chasing Mick. What he had to worry about was the shape-shifter, who would try to fool them by maybe taking on Brock's form or one of the guys.

Smell. He just needed to remember to sniff.

He heard Grizz roar, and his own furious sound answered his packmate.

He knew Grizz's scent, and it was Rey who was with him. They just needed to rendezvous and find Brock.

He crashed the door, following Brock's scent—the trail was so bright it almost hurt his eyes. Greg had done his best to make it easy for him, and for that, he was grateful.

Rey ran ahead, moving right for Dylan, who was in wolf form, which worked like a charm, because Grizz was with him, and they had to work together.

Bear work.

Grizz roared, and the metal buildings shuddered.

They thundered through, hearing a shout behind them as a guard engaged Dylan and Rey. He and Locke kept moving. Their team had this.

They needed to save Brock.

TWELVE

Mick finally doubled back on himself, making a run for the warehouse James had given him the coordinates to, this time in wolf form.

He could hear the sirens, and he'd seen the cop cars and the big black SUVs going by. The cops and the Feds were on the way. All he had to do was keep up with Kit in his mind and not let his bear down.

Kit was on the move, the thoughts pure ursine, a dull, blunt fury. It was a glorious sensation, in the strangest way. He loved the life, the focus, the power inherent in his bear.

Kit the human was sweet, kind, a medic, and a fixer. Kit the bear was pure mama bear, for want of a better phrase. A fierce protector.

He came up to Dylan and Rey, his packmate defending their fox against three attackers. He knew Kit was with Locke, their grizzly in top form, so as much as it killed him, he stopped to even the score.

Once Dylan saw him, the tide began to turn, and they fought as a pack, Rey joining with them. What he lacked in brute strength, Rey made up in speed, darting here and there, tossing kidney punches. They left their opponents in a heap on the floor, and they headed through a series of doors that had been utterly destroyed.

His bears were on it.

When they ran in, they ended up with their noses almost up bear butts.

There was a standoff, Greg crumpled unconscious on the floor, and two Brocks holding each other off at gunpoint.

Fuck him.

He wanted to encourage Kit, but he didn't want his mate distracted. Not now.

Not at all.

Fuck him.

Hush, boss. Working.

Use your nose. He probably didn't need to remind Kit of that.

Brock is on my right.

Mick let his nose and ears and eyes all work in concert, and sure enough, Brock was the one who was actually bleeding, who was breathing hard from being injured, and who smelled like rage, not fear.

That was a damn fine call on Kit's part, and he knew Grizz had to know as well.

Whether fox and wolf behind him did was another matter. He couldn't make a move to indicate it either. Not without giving away that he knew and getting someone shot.

When Kit and Grizz moved, it was a stunning sight—Grizz went to cover Brock, while Kit charged for the other one, a shot ringing out a heartbeat before Kit swiped, the fake-Brock's head separating neatly from his body.

Mick leaped forward, wanting to make sure Kit wasn't shot. *Mate! Tell me you're okay.* He needed to hear it. Now.

I think so. Kit's head came up, and he looked back at the door. *Someone is coming.*

It had better be the damn cops. Mick was ready to be done with this shit.

No shit. I've had all the fun I'm looking to have.

Come on. We need to get Greg up just in case it's not the good guys. He sniffed Kit as surreptitiously as he could for blood.

Broken wrist. Hurts like a bitch. Kit looked at Greg and roared.

Greg moaned, his hands opening and closing. He looked like he'd been mauled pretty badly. Mick went to paw at him, urging him to get up. Greg popped up, his eyes black as the raven he was for a moment, then going the more human dark brown. "Shit. Hartness. That really you?"

He barked. *Come on, man. Time to move. Now. Now.*

Mick knew Greg couldn't understand him, but it didn't matter. The urgency had to come through.

Greg stood, unsteady, and then a huge raven was there. Boom. Yeah. Greg could fly. That was awesome for him. They needed to get moving.

When the team burst into room, though, it was Feds, led by Cole Matthews. "I hope to god none of you is that shape-shifter. And I'm going to need someone to give me the damn sitrep. Now. The building is secure."

Kit stared right through Cole and rumbled, the sound pure warning. Do. Not. Fuck. With. The. Bear.

"Yeah, yeah, big guy. Not that it helps, because you're a bear."

Brock climbed out from under a pile of grizzly. "I can update you, but Maldinado is still in the wind."

"Goddamn it!" Cole snapped. "Who's the headless wonder?"

"The shape-shifter. The jaguar who was under Maldina-do's influence." Brock sighed. "I feel for him. I could have been him."

Kit's lip wrinkled at the exact same time as Grizz's. Impressive.

"Thank you, amigos, for your faith in me, but it hasn't been for lack of trying."

Mick thought of his human body, and was suddenly on hands and knees, panting. "Can we debrief back at our place, Cole?"

"Yeah. Yeah, someone needs to get me some clothes for these guys so we can transport them." Cole looked frustrated as fuck, and Mick understood. "We have an armored van. You'll be as safe as you can be."

"Thanks." Mick waited for the blankets to arrive, then wrapped up. "Let me look at the vehicle." He waved to his mate. "Kit, come check it out. You sniff out the trouble."

Kit came lumbering over, nose working already. Cole let Kit sniff him, then took them out to the van. His bear worked it over.

Looks good, Mick. Tired.

He nodded, stroking the fur that was a little matted from their adventure. "I know."

No. It hurts. It really hurts.

Your head? Or your wrist? He knew both had to be bad, but Kit was their medic. They all had basics, but Kit had the touch.

Mainly the wrist. Don't tell.

But...

Kit rumbled.

I won't, but know your limits. You have to conserve your energy. He'll be coming for us. He wanted Kit safely tucked away, but that was just mate instinct.

Kit could be a huge help if there was another fight.

Hell, Kit had already beheaded someone tonight. No wonder his wrist hurt.

We get our vacay soon, baby, he reminded Kit. He believed it. This would be the last straw for Maldinado. He knew it.

Soon everyone was shifted back, with blankets and sweatpants. Brock and Rey were bruised, but Kit looked like he'd been beaten. This whole thing had been really been tough on him, and he would kill anyone who touched his mate again.

They climbed into Cole's van, and Mick took the front seat. He needed to feel like he had some control. He thought Cole felt the same way, because he drove even though he had five agents who could do it for him.

"You think he'll come for us on the road?"

"I don't know. I expected him to be here," Mick said. "So where the hell is he?"

"He had a special torture place he was setting up for Brock," Greg said, back in human form. "So he was going to leave the others here for the men to destroy, and he was going to take Brock elsewhere."

"What?" The thought of his bear destroyed made him want to roar.

"I'm just telling you what his plan was." Greg sounded worn to the bone, and he was swaying when Mick looked back at him.

"Lie down," Kit told Greg. "You need to rest. Your color sucks and your pulse is thready."

Greg kinda...fell over and Kit caught him. He'd been in the wind a long time.

"He's just exhausted," Kit said, easing him to the floorboard. "It's been a shit few months, right?"

"And then some," Cole said grimly. "I hate that we lost touch with him, but he clearly got in good with the big names in this case."

"I don't want to think what he would have to do in order to do that," Mick said. He would bet Greg never went undercover again.

"No. No, this is asinine, Mick!" Brock growled. "Just let the fucker have me."

"No way." Mick could growl too. "We haven't gone to all this damn trouble to give you up now."

"Hell no!" That was Rey, his fierce little *grr* so cool.

"We're a team, Brock," Kit said. "All of us, so suck it up."

"I will bite you, Little Bear," Brock shot back, and Kit grumbled.

"You'll try."

"Hey, Hartness, your phone. I recovered it at the crash." One of the agents handed him his mobile, which was ringing. Damn. He checked the number. Unknown. What the fuck? He let it go, not wanting to talk to anyone right now. No clients. The only call he would answer was James or Hank.

The ringing stopped, but then it started again almost immediately, with the name Maldinado popping up this time.

"What the fuck?"

He slid the answer bar over, barking into the phone. "Hartness."

"You killed my cat, so I killed yours. Both of them." The voice was heavily accented and full of venom. "I will kill you all and take Brock anyway. You are going to lose."

"Fuck you, asshole. You're bluffing." He had to be. James would have sounded some kind of alarm.

"You wish. If you don't want your bear shipped all over the world in pieces, you'll hand the jaguar over."

The spurt of rage made his blood rush in his ears. "No way. He's not yours. He belongs to us. He's part of my pack, you motherfucker." Mick had no idea what to do except keep the crazy bastard talking.

Brock snarled, lunging for the phone, and Grizz caught him and dragged his back.

"Don't you mean Jaguarfucker?" The laughter was wild, purely insane. Not crazy smart, just nuts.

"Maybe I mean pigfucker. You're a nutball, and now your toy soldier has been taken out of commission. You have to do your own dirty work, and I don't think you remember how."

"I knew enough to drug your James again." The sneer in that voice put his back up, making the hairs rise on the nape of his neck.

Fuck. He was going to lose his shit. James would never let the bastard in. Neither would Hank.

It wouldn't happen. He knew his team too well. James was either barricaded in his office, or he'd seen Maldinado coming and gotten to the new panic room bolt-hole they'd created.

"You're not getting him. Period. Ever." He kept his voice even and firm. He wasn't going to scream. Curse, sure, but not scream.

"Even if it costs you the little baby bear?"

"We go down together, you fucker." If he kept Maldinado talking, the man couldn't do anything evil.

Kit caught his gaze and nodded. *Together. You and me. Together.*

Always, baby.

Cole's head tilted, his hand going to his ear, and his eyes widened. He pulled off at the next exit, but Mick couldn't ask him what the hell he was even doing. He had to keep Maldinado on the line.

"I'll make him scream and you'll watch. I'll take him apart joint by joint. You know how long I can keep him alive?"

Cole nodded, murmuring as he found an empty parking lot, driving in lazy circles.

What the fuck? Mick made a motion with his hand, which meant just that, trying to figure out what Cole was doing? Had he lost his mind?

Cole snatched his phone from the console and started typing furiously with one hand, still moving with the other.

Mick tried to focus. Maldinado was screaming, really ramping up. He would bet spittle was flying.

Cole held up his phone.

<James & Hank in safe room. M in building. Comms secure. J&H safe.>

Shit. He sagged with relief.

Okay. Okay, time to plan.

He took Cole's phone. <Me. Sitrep>

<in the comms room. Have him following a wormhole. Foaming at the mouth>

<sez he has you. Drugs given>

<Bluff. In safe room>

"Are you hearing me, Hartness?" Maldinado screamed. His voice echoed with real madness, his words slurring with some sort of physical issue. As if he was taking his own drugs.

"I hear you, you fluffy-tailed psycho. We're coming for you. If you took my James, I will rip your ears off and sell you as a trophy."

"I'm going to make him assfuck you until you bleed!"

"Hmmm. Nah. I'm pretty resilient." He could taunt the man now that he knew his team was safe and he didn't have to worry about Maldinado's pet shape-shifter. He tapped a note to James. <Booby traps?>

<Front door. Garage bay.>

<Got it> He did. They had other ways in. Thank god James and Hank were okay. He handed Cole's phone to Kit, then made a motion to Cole to get them moving again. He'd have to hang up on Maldinado soon, but he wanted the guy foaming, ready to do hasty shit and make mistakes. He needed it, in fact, so they could get back into their building and take the fucker down.

Mick took stock while the guys silently read up on James's texts. Brock was at about fifty percent. Kit was down one hand, though he knew he would go at it hard. Dylan had a few scratches, but Rey was banged up. Locke seemed in good form.

They did have James and Hank as aces in the hole, and Cole and his men would be a help. Greg could stay with the vehicle.

Finally they were a few blocks away, and Brock leaned forward. "Guess what, monte de merda? Locke fucks me so good with his big cock that you could shove your fist in me and I'd never feel you. It would be nothing. You are nothing."

There was a long silence. Then, "I'm going to kill you all." The line went dead.

"Feel better?" Mick made sure his phone was off. "Good one, Brock. He'll be tearing his hair out trying to figure out his next move. How do you want to go in, Cole?"

Cole raised his eyebrows. "You're asking me?"

"Hey, you're the Fed."

"We need to draw him out. Have James run some video of the last drill we did. Make him believe we're in." Rey sounded sure. "He's in there, surrounded by screens. Let James fuck with his world."

"Good idea, foxy. Send it to James, Cole."

"I've opened the channel. He can hear you now that Maldinado is off the comm."

"I'll run it, boss," James said. "He hasn't discovered the garage entrance that Kit had our guy put in, the one off to the south."

"What are the traps?"

"I'm assuming they're acid—glass with a liquid, set to fall on you."

"When you get here, boss, I'll be at his tail." Hank sounded pissed.

"Stay safe until we're there. No one faces this guy totally alone. At least until we know he's unarmed and has no drugs." He glared at Brock, who gave him a wide-eyed stare.

"*Eu, hermao?* I would never."

"I will make Locke sit on you."

Brock grinned, the look vicious, the violence inherent in the expression chilling. "This ends tonight."

Mick nodded. "Yes. One way or the other. This ends tonight."

"It's Brock's kill, if possible," Locke said flatly.

Dylan nodded. "Agreed."

Mick got it. Brock needed the closure.

Kit rolled his eyes. *I've already done a shit-ton of damage.*

You are a stud, baby. But Brock gets to take Maldinado if we can help it. You did your job with the shape-shifter.

Fine with me. I want a bath, a bacon sandwich, and my bed.

Me too. Then our vacation after all the fallout is cleaned up.

He felt Kit's utter, wistful need for just that. *Just you and me.*

Just us. They had a lot of time to make up.

I want it, bad. Kit's thoughts broke off as they pulled onto their street. "Stop here. In case."

Cole pulled off, hands on the wheel, staring at the building. "Okay, Mick. Your men know the building. We go in as quiet as we can, and we split up to come at him from all directions. One of my men will go with each set of your team members."

"Greg," Mick said. "I want you to stay with the vehicle with at least one agent. Just in case things go bad and we need wheels fast."

Greg gave him a wry smile. "You saying I look too bad to go fast?"

"I said what I said."

"We won't leave you hanging. Keep comms wide open."

"You'll hear every word," Cole said. A look passed between Cole and Greg that he couldn't quite read, but then Cole reached out and shook Greg's hand hard. "Glad to see you out of that."

"Thanks. Keep your head down, asshole."

Huh. That was worth watching with interest after this was all over. Not that he was nosy. Or a matchmaker. Or anything like that.

"We need weapons."

"We can armor up in the garage, assuming he didn't find my stash," Kit said.

"He didn't," James came back. "Home movie is rolling."

"Kit, you want to take the lead or the rear," Locke asked.

"I'll take the lead."

Mick bit back a protest. It made sense to have the bears front and back. They could take more punishment, and they had strength on their side.

He just hated it.

"All right, ladies," Mick teased. "Let's do this."

It was time to take this motherfucker down.

Thirteen

Kit's nerves were right on the edge of misfiring.

He was taking point because he knew the entrance to the garage, and he knew where the weapons were stored. So he crept into the garage, his nose working. Yeah, he could smell whatever acid Maldinado had used in his trap.

Acid and drugs to burn and push into wounds. He moved quickly, tearing the door of the ammunition closet off the hinges.

Mick and Cole caught it before it hit the floor. Right. Adrenaline. He needed to calm down.

They armored up, and it felt like they were going into battle against an army, not one man. James assured them Maldinado was alone. But just in case he'd called in reinforcements after hanging up on Mick, they needed to be prepared.

Cole and Mick came with him. Dylan and Rey and two agents went up the back stairs. And Brock and Locke took one agent with them.

Kit was keeping the bear at bay, but it was a struggle. He

wanted to run up the stairs and bash away at the doors to the comms office and just end this.

That would probably lead to injury, if not death. Mad hatter as the guy was, James said Maldinado had set traps all along the way. He had to take care, use all his senses, and not get careless.

He felt Mick's hand on his back, just a ghost of a touch, but he knew Mick was basically telling him the same thing. They all needed to get out of this alive. All but one.

Then it would be over, and they could begin to heal again. Please.

They slipped up the stairs, the sounds of things breaking upstairs enough to make his lip curl.

He had to hold himself back. No rushing.

"Shit." James's voice came through. They all had earbuds now from the armory cabinet. "One of the agents got hit with some sort of glass container full of unknown substance. He's down. Dylan and Rey are intact."

"Where?"

"Stairs. Watch the landing."

Fuck. Okay, he could handle that. He slowed down, taking care not to rush this. The landing they hit on the front stairs was blocked, and he had a feeling it was like a puzzle. Like Jenga. If they pulled the wrong piece out, something would crash down on them.

That would suck pretty bad, and he spared a good thought for the agent with the wolf and fox. Hopefully down didn't mean dead.

They disarmed the trap in between the second and third floors, and they barely missed getting burned by one midway up.

"Jesus," Cole murmured. "He couldn't have been here this long."

"He's nuts," Mick said. "He's like some kind of energizer bunny of evil."

Kit snorted. "Yeah. He's something all right. Okay, we're hitting your office level, James."

"He's barricaded, and I've got him. He's watching the screen with Brock on it like he's mesmerized. He's caught by it. You have the element of surprise."

"Good deal." Mick took a deep breath. "Check in."

"We're at the landing on the office level," Dylan said.

"We're here." Brock's voice was in person, not in his earbud. "Blow the fucking door."

Mick pushed past him, because his mate was far better with explosives. "I want the cats in the rear, just in case. He has an endless supply of that stupid Peaches drug that took you all down," Mick snarled. "No arguing."

Bossy mate. He and Locke stood between Mick and the felines, though, didn't they?

Mick was the alpha and they were the pack, even if they weren't all wolves.

Mick carefully checked the seals on the door, sniffing at the handle, then setting a series of charges. He motioned them all back, a little battery-operated detonator in hand.

"Let's do this, guys."

Kit lowered his head and lifted his weapon. He was ready.

———

Mick blew the damn lock, and all he could smell was ozone. No poison, no acid. Looked like Maldinado hadn't wanted to take a chance on hurting himself in case anyone got this far. Or maybe he just figured no one would make it up to the inner sanctum.

They burst into James and Rey's tech paradise, guns

drawn, ready to blaze away. Maldinado whirled around to face them, eyes widening, jaw going slack.

"No! No, you are still on the lower level."

That was pure, unadulterated panic. Hoo yeah. Element of surprise, for sure.

The bastard was bald and gaunt, eyes red-rimmed and wild. That was shocking enough, given his intel had Maldinado as a fairly good-sized, healthy fox. Now he looked like he'd been in some third world prison for a decade, his facial bones standing out, his eyes hollow and bruised.

Worse than anything was the smell.

The son of a bitch was rotting from within, and he smelled like the distinct peaches drug he'd created, along with unwashed body and blood.

Maldinado reached for a bag that sat on a chair, and Kit moved like a half-shifted black blur, one mostly clawed paw shooting out and obliterating Maldinado's hand.

Screaming, Maldinado scrambled back, arm clutched to his chest, blood dripping down over his shirt.

"Oops," Kit said around a mouthful of bear teeth.

"No tricks, dickhead. I'll let the bear take you apart like you promised to do to him." Mick waved his gun happily, and Cole darted over to grab the bag, moving it out of reach. Maldinado didn't move and was pretty much moaning and holding his arm.

"Brock, help me. They're hurting me." The appeal was so damn pathetic, as if the bastard had any right to ask anything of Brock. Ever.

Brock's lips curled. "Are they? Shame. Maybe it's time you feel what it's like to be a little tortured."

Those crazy eyes seemed to glow for a moment, and Mick could see the charisma that made people follow this guy. It was all but burnt out now, and it explained a lot about why this asshole's organization was falling apart.

Maldinado couldn't hold it together if he was going to pieces.

"You're mine. You're mine and you always have been, you nasty little fuck. You're all mine." Maldinado became more shrill with every word, his cheeks flushing in his gray-skinned face.

Mick's lip curled, but he didn't have to answer. Brock did, by turning and kissing Locke passionately.

Maldinado sprang, but Kit caught him. "Sit down and shut up. Not so scary without your dozens of henchmen."

Mick smiled, feeling fucking amazing. "You're losing them all. That's why you're here alone. You're running out of people to follow you, aren't you? You should have kept your pet shape-shifter by your side instead of trusting him not to commit suicide by bear."

Maldinado growled, and before he could move, pulled out a syringe, holding it to Kit's throat, teeth bared. "I want Brock."

"Fuck you," Kit growled. "You can't have him." Kit was vibrating, and Mick's finger went tense on the trigger, but he couldn't squeeze off a shot. Fox hiding behind bear. There was no way he wouldn't hit Kit.

"I'll make him suffer, lover. You know I will."

Brock stared at Kit, eyes green as emerald, then he turned away. "Who cares? I have my bear."

Mick heard the drawl in Brock's voice, and he suddenly got it. Bear.

Let the bear come, mate. Let him out in a rush.

I don't think I can... I'm tired.

Do it! Now!

Mick poked Kit mentally, just like he was tossing a little jolt of electricity. He needed Kit out of the way. Safe. No one could beat berserker bear, and Maldinado stood no chance against their berserker.

I love you. Kit went from zero to one twenty in seconds. No one had ever been able to shift so quickly, to go from gentle medic to furious ursine in a rush.

It worked. The syringe flew one way, Maldinado the other, and the sound of Kit's fury shook the earth.

Brock answered with a snarl, his rarely seen jaguar form blurring as he leaped at Maldinado.

Kit batted the syringe away with one paw and it slammed into the wall across the room.

Maldinado shifted into this awful, broken half-being, the poison dripping from him, and Mick realized in that moment that no one could save the beast. No one. "Kit. Come on."

Kit roared.

"No. This is Brock's." Brock was already on Maldinado, his jaws clamped over the fox's face. Smothering him. It was the kindest damn thing to do. There was no way Maldinado would survive to go to prison, let alone make it a week once inside. "Come with me, mate. Right now." He put one hand on Kit's fuzzy neck. "Let's go get James and Hank."

They turned their backs on Brock and his lover and Maldinado. Cole stayed. There had to be at least one witness.

"I have medical on the way," James said in his ear. "Two agents are injured. Dylan and Rey are coming back around to meet you. The back-office entrance will need your bomb squad self."

"Kit's hurt. He needs medical as well. Greg's outside in rough shape."

"But it's over, boss? You swear? It's over?"

"It's all over but the cleanup. I'll get a hold of Pope to help. He knows some crime-scene cleanup people."

"Thank god." That came from Hank. "I'm done with this shit, man."

"You and all of us. Kit needs a doctor. Now." He stopped in the hallway where Kit simply collapsed, exhausted. "Shit."

"I'll send medical toward you. Cole and Greg made sure friendly guys are on the way. Do I need to do any cleanup?"

"I'll send Dylan and Rey to close up the armory in the garage. The rest is just watching for those traps he put in until we get them cleaned up."

"Get to work then, boss. I've got eyes on the bear."

I don't want to leave you.

Just tired. Go. Kit's mental voice was weak but there. *You owe me two more days of vacay.*

I owe you my soul, mate.

I love you.

He sank down to rest his forehead against Kit's, then stood. "I need to get shit done."

Kit rumbled for him, then nudged him on his way.

Yeah. Maldinado was dead, damn it. It was time to clean house.

Fourteen

Kit slept, and whenever he woke up, he closed his eyes and fell back asleep.

Everything in his entire body hurt, and he groaned whenever he moved. He had shifted more in a day than he had in weeks, and the explosion had damn near rattled his brain out of his head. The adrenaline hadn't helped.

Maybe he would wake up someday.

When he woke up again, his nose started working, the smell of soup strong on the air.

"You're going to get up, mate. You need to eat and talk to me."

Mick. Mick couldn't make soup without opening a can, but this smelled homemade. Maybe Rey? That was sweet.

"Clam chowder, love. Rey made it. James made grilled cheese with brie and raspberry jam too. Just for you." Mick waved a plate under his nose.

Oh, there was honey...

"Everyone's okay?" Brock and Locke and everyone?

"Everyone is good. The two injured agents will recover, though one had the same reaction to the drugs as James. Greg is down, but he was on the edge of a breakdown, and he's kind of a birdbrain. He'll be fine."

Kit snorted. Birdbrain. He liked what Mick did there.

"Good. It's over. He's gone?"

"Yeah. Ironically, he was so diseased from taking a concoction of his own drugs that he could have keeled over any minute."

Kit cracked one eye open. "Life can go back to normal?"

"Nope." Mick grinned cheerfully at him, even though he had a huge bruise on his left cheek. Kit would bet it had smacked the window in their crash, if it was still that lurid. "First, we go on vacation. Dylan is running the PI cases, and Brock is talking about offering bodyguard services. Oh, and Cole and Greg want a big old debrief session to justify shit to their bosses."

"Okay. When we get home, right?" He reached out, stroking Mick's arm. Dude. He had a cast.

"Yeah. Your wrist was bad, baby. Shattered. The medic was a raccoon shifter. He said your body would need some help while you were healing." Mick lifted his hand and kissed his fingers, which stuck out of the cast.

"Mmm. It doesn't ache too bad, so I bet it comes off soon."

"Do you think you can sit up and have a bite? You need some fuel. They gave you two bags of fluid while you were asleep."

"Has it been long?"

"Six days." Mick winked at him. "Hibernating bear."

"Oh, man." Kit popped up, then moaned as his whole body protested. "Whoa. Right. I was beat up."

"Yes. I was worried, but I kept hearing you, so I knew you would be okay." Mick sat, tearing off a piece of sandwich to feed him.

He snapped it up, and suddenly he was hungry, his belly snarling.

Mick fed him, bite by bite, spoon by spoon. He loved each flavor. The brie was creamy, the fruit and honey tart and sweet, and the soup had a briny sea flavor. He could have kept going, but then his belly cramped a little, and he sat back.

"You did good, baby. Perfect."

"I'm sorry, I was... I couldn't wake up all the way." He'd been exhausted, deeper than the bone.

"I know. You'll sleep some more, but this was good. For you to eat. Next time you wake up, we can have a shower." Mick paused, petting his hair. "You did me proud, Kit. You saved the fucking day."

"That's all I wanted. To make you proud." He'd wanted to prove himself.

"You did. I knew you were good, love. I did. I was just scared to put you out front." Mick touched his cast. "I didn't want stuff like this to happen."

He nodded. What could he say?

"How's Brock? Mentally, I mean."

"Shell-shocked. I think he's been running so long from this that he can't believe it's over. Locke is like, dancing."

Kit chuckled. "I bet he is. I would be."

"Do you mind if I come in, rest with you?" Mick sounded hesitant, and Kit snorted.

"Never. It's our bed."

"I just didn't want to hurt you."

Kit scooted over. "More like I was taking up all the space. Have you eaten?"

"I had two bowls of the soup and a ham sandwich." Mick slid in next to him. He tugged the covers over them.

"Mmm..." Kit wasn't sure if he was humming over the food or the warmth of Mick next to him. One way or the other he felt like he would heal faster if he absorbed Mick's heat and care. He loved having Mick here with him.

"Better?" Mick asked.

"Yeah. I was missing you and I didn't know it."

"I did," Mick said, sounding so much more like his normal self. He'd been too damn sweet this whole time.

His wolf was gruff and tough. An alpha. That was what he needed most of the time. Kit cuddled in, happier now.

"You sound better, babe. Less bear and more Kit."

"Was I a little lost?"

"A little. Now I know you're with me all the way." Mick kissed his mouth. "Sleep, baby. I'll be here when you wake up."

"Promise?"

"Even if I have to piss." Mick laughed at his own joke and Kit bit him.

"That you can go for a few seconds if you need to."

"Thanks, baby. That's generous."

He pinched Mick's nipple. "More sleeping. Less talking."

Kit pretended to snore, really ripping them, and Mick began to chuckle, his lover's laughter filling the air.

Okay, that was...amazing.

Kit grinned, and he couldn't be more pleased. He'd done that.

Mick was still laughing when he fell asleep again.

———

Mick knew he needed to have a meeting. A real one, with the whole team. Greg had been staying with them, and Cole had just happened to drop by with a couple of boxes of donuts and bagel sandwiches, so it was time to assemble the team.

Which meant pounding on doors, because a text they could ignore, but him in person, bellowing, they couldn't.

Dylan and Rey came down from upstairs, attached at the hips.

Brock and Locke were a little harder.

He kept knocking. "I know you two can hear me. I need you in on this, guys!"

Brock came to the door, snarling softly. "What do you want, man?"

"I need us all to meet before Kit and I go out of town. Less than an hour, I promise, and Kit is making mac and cheese and sausages."

"You got him to cook again, did you?" Brock's nostrils twitched, though, because he did love sausages.

"I did. Well, he volunteered. He likes that part. He's a nurturer." That was so damn true.

"He is. He's ours. We're coming. We want yummies."

"Okay, cool. No formal wear required," he teased. "Pants would be good though."

Brock just flipped him off.

James and Hank were easy. They were asleep in the office, curled in the corner as kitties. "Guys. Food and meeting in the common."

James yawned, showing off all those teeth.

"Mac and cheese, kitty."

Hank uncurled, stretching and yawning, too, but obviously interested.

"Come on, guys. I'm asking, not ordering, but I need you there."

James wandered over to him, nuzzled his hip, then nodded.

"Thanks, man." He rubbed James's ears. "I know everyone deserves a break, but I want us on the same page before Kit and I head off."

James headbutted him, and he headed downstairs. It

didn't take long before everyone was there, and Kit was filling plates.

"Smells good, baby. Do I need to do anything?"

Kit almost dropped a plate. "Did you offer to help?"

He swatted Kit's butt. "Shut up and feed me, you."

Kit's laughter echoed deep in his soul, and that little wiggle after the slap had Mick growling happily. Damn.

Cole and Greg came in, too, Greg still moving very carefully. "Wow, something smells amazing."

"You guys haven't eaten with us yet," Mick said. "We have some good feeds."

"We do." Locke took his plate. "Best thing about working here—tater tots on demand."

"Mmm." Rey grinned. "Tots."

"You do good tots," Kit agreed. He looked tickled to see the whole pack.

They all got plates and settled, all of them looking to him as they began to eat.

Mick grinned a little, waiting until first servings were almost done. Then he cleared his throat.

"So. Cole, you want to fill us in on the situation with Maldinado's organization?"

Cole nodded easily. "Scattered and shattered. The whole thing collapsed. Without Hetrick, the drug production was mostly out of commission anyway. Patel had been supplying the guy with real estate, and he was running out of safe houses. And the shape-shifter guy was the one hiring the flunkies. They've scattered like rats." He shrugged. "No one will be coming after you."

"Thank goodness. Brock's earned a rest," Kit murmured. "So it's really finished."

"Graças a Deus," Brock growled softly.

"Yeah. I'm done with this shit," Greg said. "That guy was a nutball."

Cole snorted. "And a half. Anyway, I'm on administrative leave pending an investigation because I pulled a police captain off his post and put him undercover for a task force that wasn't sanctioned by the higher-ups."

Mick nodded. "And Greg is...here for a while." The man needed a home—physically and emotionally.

Greg nodded, lips tight. "Hank gets it. Undercover can do a number on a guy."

They all just left that at that.

"Thank you, Cole Matthews," Brock said. "I didn't know you were helping us on your own."

"Guys like that need to be off the street. The higher-ups don't necessarily see crimes against shifters as an issue."

"I do." Brock's eyes flashed gold. "I want to offer personal protection services. If I had all the resources, I would."

Kit blinked. "You're loaded. What else do you need?"

Brock laughed. "Ah, irmão. Many things. People I trust to do the work for one."

"You have Locke."

"I'd buy in, Brock," Cole said. "I'm tired of the bullshit politics. I just want to help."

"Me too." Greg shrugged. "The department has offered to settle so I leave. And I get to keep all I've put into my retirement."

"I have thoughts. Dylan can take over running the PI business. You guys could start this new venture, and I'll help bankroll it and get all your stuff together. Permits. You know." Mick grinned at Brock, then Dylan. "I'd be happy to just be a facilitator."

Kit rumbled softly and stood, standing to take his plate to the kitchen.

Silly bear.

What? I'm back to taking pictures at sleazy hotels?

Would you trust me? "Kit will be off the roster on the PI

front as he's going to be the facilities manager. Anything we need will go through Kit. Not just the motor pool, but medical, housing, weapons, and expenses."

Kit blinked, and a surprised pleasure hit him like a wave. *Seriously? You mean it?*

"Dude! Go Kit! Facilities managers for, what? The Apex Corporation?" Rey's eyes were huge. "How cool!"

"Yeah. Are you and James willing to do tech for both, Rey? James?" Mick was already loving being a business owner and delegating.

"Sure, boss. You know I don't sleep," James answered, and Hank's low growl was sure and sharp.

"He can't work all the time."

"Rey either," Dylan added. "We need more help."

"We do. More PIs, people to do the bodyguard work, and at least one more tech guru. You guys know people. Put the feelers out." He met every set of eyes. "We're a pack. I want to keep us together."

Brock chuffed softly. "Such an alpha. Always growing his pack."

He shrugged. It was his instinct, his calling. This was his insane family, and he loved them all, especially his beloved, patient, nurturing mate.

"So are we all willing to make this a plan under the Apex umbrella?"

Hank chuckled. "As long as I just get to be a gumshoe."

"Ditto," Dylan said with a grin. "I like it simple."

"You got it." That he could promise.

"I'm in." Greg sounded hopeful. "I might need a month or two, just to breathe and heal, but I'm in."

Me too. Kit's thought was a sweet caress.

"We have time. Kit and I are going on vacation. Anyone else who wants to has the time off. Or if you want to be as normal as possible, we have some clients who want us to do the job." He didn't care. He was going to be out of pocket in the mountains with his bear.

"You're really going?" Dylan looked shocked. "I've never seen you actually take a vacation."

"We need time to bond. Alone." He reached up as Kit walked close behind him, hands on his shoulders.

"You do. We all need a few weeks of downtime, hmm?" Locke rumbled softly, the big grizzly looking settled in his bones. "Go take your mate away. Everything will be here for you when you come home."

"Then we plan world domination." He winked. "Thanks, guys. There's plenty of leftovers."

"The mac and cheese is amazing, Kit," Greg said. "Thanks."

"You're welcome. Make sure you make a list, you and Cole both, of your favorite foods and what you need for your rooms, and I'll deal with them." Kit smiled, and his mate looked overjoyed. "After I get back."

Cole's eyes glittered. "I like the vibe around here, man."

"Good deal." Mick stood. "Come on, baby. We have packing to do."

"Dylan, make sure someone does the dishes, please?" Kit asked.

"You got it, buddy."

Dylan and Rey would if no one else volunteered. They were solid.

He wasn't going to stress it. He was going to pack a bag and put his bear in the truck and head north.

Time to go to Canada.

Fifteen

Banff was beautiful. Utterly gorgeous.

They rented a little cabin out in the middle of the mountains, and Kit was over the moon.

The snow was going to be here before they left, but right now, it was just perfect. Hell, he was a bear from Colorado. Snow would be perfect.

"Mmm. Are you wandering, bear?" Mick rumbled from the bed.

"Admiring the scenery, mate." He turned toward Mick, his attention caught and captured.

"Yeah? Anymore moose?"

They'd seen moose the day they arrived. They were so damn cool and Mick had been like a little kid.

"Not this morning. I did see a mountain lion though. She was happy."

"Was she? Good. That's happy making." Mick sat up, sheets sliding away from him, and held out a hand.

Kit's mouth went dry, and he went right over, because what else could he possibly do? This was his mate, his partner, his lover, his soul.

They'd been very busy being tourists and loving each other, and yes, bonding. He could hear Mick so clearly now. Feel the love Mick had for him.

The time to go home was getting closer. Everyday Kit was thinking about Apex, about the guys, about getting back to life and the real world.

"Are you craving cheeseburger time with the guys, baby?" Mick teased.

"I am." He cuddled in. "This has been perfect, but I'm ready to be with our pack. I know you are too. You're dreaming about them." And it felt good, to be on the same page.

"Yeah. Yeah. We're pretty relaxed, I'd say." Mick pulled him down, fingers trailing over his skin.

"We are. This has been...perfect." He'd loved every second of it, from the food to the adventure to the amazing sex.

"It has. What should we have for supper tonight? Should we go into town?" Mick was just... Zen. It was stunning.

"Mmm...that fish place with the honey-miso-glazed salmon?"

"That sounds good." Mick liked their steaks, and they could split some sort of appetizer. Just to go out without worry was such a wonderful thing. He hoped the other guys were getting out more too.

"We don't have to go out already though..." He was spoiled now, having access to Mick's body whenever he wanted it.

"Nope. Not for a long while. We have munchies. Lube..."

"The important things." They had a few days left, and they could go out anytime. "Kiss me?"

"Mmmm." Mick pulled him down for a kiss, licking at his lips, then nipping before diving in.

He held on tight. Sometimes he couldn't believe this was real, but those thoughts came less and less often. Mick had shown him over and over, starting with trusting him to take on Maldinado, right up until now, when Mick let him straddle those lean hips so he could ride if he wanted.

Kit had wanted nothing but this—Mick's love, his respect, his hunger. Now that he had it, his dreams were coming true, and it was better than he'd dreamed. He felt, finally, like Mick's partner.

He was so in love it hurt.

Good. Your love is the best thing that's ever happened to me. Thank you for waiting for me.

Thank you for seeing me. Finally.

Mick smiled up at him, and they had finally come to the place Kit had known they could find.

They were a team. All of them and just the two of them.

They were Apex Investigations.

The End

Want More?

Julia Talbot

Join the Spurs and Shifters Newsletter for free stories, news, and contests from Julia Talbot and BA Tortuga!

https://lp.constantcontact.com/su/A9CRUzp/baandjulia

Afterword

Hey, folks!

Thanks so much for reading my book! I'm so glad you made it here. If you liked the book, I hope you'll consider leaving a rating or review at your retailer of choice or adding the book to your Goodreads shelf.

If you're interested in more of my books, or in news about when they come out and what's coming soon, please check out my Facebook Group https://www.facebook.com/groups/juliatalbot/ or my newsletter here: https://lp.constantcontact.com/su/A9CRUzp/baandjulia

XXOO and Keep reading!

Julia Talbot

ALSO BY JULIA TALBOT

Alpha Tales

An Alpha in Sheep's Clothing

Packmate for Hire

Too Many Alphas

Apex Investigations

Fox and Wolf

Jaguar and Grizzly

Mountain Lion and Bobcat

Alpha and Bear

Apex Security

Solids and Stripes

Dead and Breakfast

Fangs and Catnip

Fangs for the Memories

Home for the Howlidays

Full Moon Dating

New Moon

Isaiah and Jameson

Grizzly List

Bear Wanted

One and Only Bear

Bearly Working

Midnight Rodeo
Big Bear, Little Bear
Light a Rocket
Vampire Protection
The Dragon's Dilemma
Up in Flames

Nose to Tail, Inc.
Wolfmanny
Wolf's Man Friday
Wolf Maneuvers

The Peculiars
The Curse of the Mummy's Heart
The Shadow of the Count

Riding Cowboy Flats
Jackass Flats
Just a Cowboy
Riding the Circuit

Summit Springs
High Side

* * *

Contemporary
Catching Heir
Chef on Chef

Drive Your Truck

Home for the Hollandaise

Jumping, Landing, and Taking

Loose Snow

Love Dot Com

One More Yule Log

Out of the Frying Pan

Perfect

Sparkle and Shine

Historical

A Gentleman of Substance

A Pirate's Paradise

Offerings

Partners on the Trail

Post Obsession

Remembering Pleasure

To Hell You Ride

The White City

Paranormal

Bad Dog

Blue Moon Bar

Faster Bobcat

Link to the Crescent

Night of the Living Manny

Pack Mates

The Fire Inside

Thorns

Tomb of the God King

Touching Evil

About the Author

Julia Talbot lives in the great Southwest with her wife and four basset hounds. A full-time author, Julia writes paranormals and more with lots of love and action and, as her alter ego Minerva Howe, she writes mpreg and alpha/omega stories. She believes that everyone deserves a happy ending, so she writes about love without limits, where all of her stories leave a mark.

Visit Julia's website: http://www.juliatalbot.com

9 798822 400440